indian horse

INDIAN

richard wagamese

HORSE

a novel

Douglas & McIntyre

Douglas and McIntyre (2013) Ltd.
PO Box 219
Madeira Park, BC Canada V0N 2H0
www.douglas-mcintyre.com

Cataloguing data available from Library and Archives Canada
ISBN 978-1-55365-402-5 (pbk.)
ISBN 978-1-55365-970-9 (ebook)

Editing by Barbara Pulling
Copyediting by Peter Norman
Cover and text design by Jessica Sullivan
Cover photographs: (clockwise from top left) Photography Collection, Miriam & Ira D. Wallach Division of Art, Prints and Photographs, the New York Public Library, Astor Lenox and Tilden Foundations; iStock; Carl Iwasaki/Getty Images
Printed and bound in Canada by Friesens
Text printed on acid-free paper

We gratefully acknowledge the financial support of the Canada Council for the Arts, the British Columbia Arts Council, the Province of British Columbia through the Book Publishing Tax Credit and the Government of Canada through the Canada Book Fund for our publishing activities.

Winner of CODE's 2013 Burt Award for First Nations, Inuit and Métis Young Adult Literature

Acknowledgements

IT TAKES SOME doing to bring a book into the world. Despite the solitary seat at the desk or table, none of us ever really do it alone. I know I don't. I never have. This book took an awful lot of doing, and it was helped immeasurably by the editing prowess of Barbara Pulling and the indefatigable loyalty of my agent, John Pearce of Westwood Creative Artists. Also, the Canada Council for the Arts for the helping hand, Chris Labonté at Douglas & McIntyre for believing, the Truth and Reconciliation Commission for being there for the survivors of Canada's residential schools, and Justice Murray Sinclair for the friendship and the example. To Bebo, Juke, Johnny, Star, Josephine C., Kenny O., Peter R., Hank T., I have never forgotten your stories and your experiences with the schools. Even if you're gone now, the spirit of them, and you, are here somewhere. Miigwetch. To the Bears, Chiefs, Spirit, Wolves, Bandits and all the unnamed Native hockey teams that taught me the joy and exhilaration of the game and the shining glory of the rink, a tap on the shin pads and a whack on the fanny for the gift. To my wingers, Bob Lee, Ron Ste. Marie, Ron Tronson, Peter Mutrie and Vaughan

Begg, thanks for helping me keep my stick on the ice and my feet moving toward the goal always. To Nancy Mutrie, Wanda Tronson, Jennifer Ste. Marie, Pam Lee, Blanca Schorcht and Shelagh Rogers, heartfelt gratitude for the loyalty through the slumps and the celebrations. But mostly, to my wife, Debra Powell, who shows me every day how to be a winner, you are the shining glory of my life.

———

*For my wife, Debra Powell, for allowing me
to bask in her light and become more.*

———

I come into the peace of wild things
who do not tax their lives with forethought
of grief. I come into the presence of still water.
And I feel above me the day-blind stars
waiting with their light. For a time
I rest in the grace of the world, and am free.

WENDELL BERRY, "The Peace of Wild Things"

1 ———

My name is Saul Indian Horse. I am the son of Mary Mandamin and John Indian Horse. My grandfather was called Solomon so my name is the diminutive of his. My people are from the Fish Clan of the northern Ojibway, the *Anishinabeg,* we call ourselves. We made our home in the territories along the Winnipeg River, where the river opens wide before crossing into Manitoba after it leaves Lake of the Woods and the rugged spine of northern Ontario. They say that our cheekbones are cut from those granite ridges that rise above our homeland. They say that the deep brown of our eyes seeped out of the fecund earth that surrounds the lakes and marshes. The Old Ones say that our long straight hair comes from the waving grasses that thatch the edges of bays. Our feet and hands are broad and flat and strong, like the paws of a bear. Our ancestors learned to travel easily through territories that the *Zhaunagush,* the white man, later feared and sought our help to navigate. Our talk rolls and tumbles like the rivers that served as our roads. Our legends tell of how we emerged from the womb of our Mother the Earth; Aki is the name we have for her. We sprang forth intact, with Aki's heartbeat thrumming in our ears, prepared to become her stewards and protectors.

When I was born our people still talked this way. We had not yet stepped beyond the influence of our legends. That was a border my generation crossed, and we pine for a return that has never come to be.

These people here want me to tell my story. They say I can't understand where I'm going if I don't understand where I've been. The answers are within me, according to them. By telling our stories, hardcore drunks like me can set ourselves free from the bottle and the life that took us there. I don't give a shit about any of that. But if it means getting out of this place quicker, then telling my story is what I will do.

It was social workers at the hospital who sent me here. The New Dawn Centre. They call it a treatment facility. The counsellors here say Creator and the Grandmothers and the Grandfathers want me to live. They say a lot of things. In fact, they talk all the time, and they expect us to do the same. They sit there with their eyes all shiny and wet and hopeful, thinking we don't see them waiting. Even with my eyes on my shoes I can feel them. They call it sharing. It's one of our ancient tribal principles as Ojibway people, they claim. Many hearts beating together makes us stronger. That's why they put us in the sharing circle.

There are at least thirty of us staying here. Everyone from kids in their late teens to a few in their thirties, like me, and one woman who's so old she can't talk much anymore. We sit in circles all day. I tire of talk. It wearies me. It makes me wish for a drink. But I endure it, and when my counsellor, Moses, ushers me into his office for one-on-one time, I endure that too. I've been here a month, after six weeks in the hospital, and that's the longest I've been without a drink for years, so I guess there's some use to it. My body feels stronger. My head is clear. I eat heartily. But now, they say, the time has come for the hardest work. "If we want to live at peace with ourselves, we need to tell our stories."

I can't tell mine in the circle. I know that. There's too much to sort out and sift through. And I've noticed the younger ones getting all twitchy in their seats the few times I've tried to speak. Maybe they don't believe me, or something about what I'm saying pisses them off. Either way, I can't talk there. So Moses gave me permission to write things down. So I will. Then I'll get on with life. Somewhere.

Our people have rituals and ceremonies meant to bring us vision. I have never participated in any of them, but I have seen things. I have been lifted up and out of this physical world into a place where time and space have a different rhythm. I always remained within the borders of this world, yet I had the eyes of one born to a different plane. Our medicine people would call me a seer. But I was in the thrall of a power I never understood. It left me years ago, and the loss of that gift has been my greatest sorrow. Sometimes it feels as though I have spent my entire life on a trek to rediscover it.

—— 2

I wasn't there the day the first Indian horse came to our people, but I heard the story so many times as a boy that it became real to me.

The Ojibway were not people of the horse. Our land existed as an untamed thing, lakes, rivers, bogs and marshes surrounded by citadels of bush and rock and the labyrinthine weave of country. We had no need of maps to understand it. We were people of the *manitous*. The beings that shared our time and place were lynx, wolf, wolverine, bear, crane, eagle, sturgeon, deer, moose. The horse was a spirit dog meant to run in open places. There was no word for it in the old talk until my great-grandfather brought one back from Manitoba.

When the sun was warm and the song of the wind could be heard in the rustle of the trees, our people said that the *Maymaygwayseeuk,* the water spirits, had come out to dance. That's the kind of day it was. Sparkling. The eyes of the spirits winking off the water.

My great-grandfather had wandered off into the bite of the north wind one day near the end of winter, headed west to the land of our cousins, the Ojibway of the plains. His name was *Shabogeesick.* Slanting Sky. He was a shaman and a trapper, and because he spent so much time out on the land, it told him things, spoke to him of mysteries and teachings. They say he had the sending thought, the great gift of the original teachers. It was a powerful medicine, allowing vital teachings to be shared among people separated by tremendous distance. Shabogeesick was one of the last to claim its energy before history trampled it under foot. The land called to him one day and he walked off without a word to anyone. No one worried. It was something he did all the time.

But that late spring afternoon when he walked back out of the bush from the east, he was leading a strange black animal by a rope halter. Our people had never seen such a creature, and they were afraid. It was massive. Huge as a moose, but without antlers, and the sound of its hoofs on the ground was that of drums. It was like a great wind through a fissure in rock. People shrank from the sight of it.

"What manner of being is this?" they asked. "Do you eat it?"

"How does it come to walk beside a man? Is it a dog? Is it a grandfather who lost his way?"

The people had many questions. None would approach the animal and when it lowered its head and began to graze on the grass, they gasped.

"It is like a deer."

"Is it as gentle as *Waywashkeezhee?*"

"It is called a horse," Shabogeesick told them. "In the land of our cousins it is used to travel long distances, to bear loads too heavy for men, to warn of Zhaunagush before he can be seen."

"Horse," the people said in unison. The big animal lifted its head and whinnied, and they were afraid.

"Does it mock us?" they asked.

"It announces itself," Shabogeesick said. "It comes bearing great teachings."

He'd brought the animal back on the train and walked it thirty miles from the station to our camp on the Winnipeg River. It was a Percheron. A draught horse. A working beast, and Shabogeesick showed the people how to halter it, to rig it with straps sewn from cedar roots and trading post rope so it could haul the carcasses of moose and bear many miles out of the bush. Children learned to ride on its broad back. The horse pulled elders on toboggans across the deep snows of winter and allowed men to cut trees and haul the logs to the river where they would float them to the mill for money. Horse was indeed a gift and the people called him *Kitchi-Animoosh*. Great Dog.

Then one day Shabogeesick called everyone together in a circle on the teaching rocks where the Old Ones drew stories on the stone. The people were only ever called to those sacred stones when something vital needed to be shared. No one knows where that place is today. Of all the things that would die in the change to come, the way to that sacred place was perhaps the most grievous loss. Shabogeesick had brought Kitchi-Animoosh, and Horse nibbled at the succulent leaves of the aspen while my great-grandfather spoke.

"When the horse first called to me, I did not understand the message," Shabogeesick told them. "I had not heard that voice before. But our cousins on the plains spoke to me of the goodness of this Being, and I fasted and prayed in the sacred sweat lodge for many days to learn to speak with it.

"When I emerged from the sweat lodge this Horse was

there. I walked with it upon the plains and the Horse offered me its teachings.

"A great change will come. It will come with the speed of lightning and it will scorch all our lives. This is what Horse said to me under that great bowl of sky. 'The People will see many things they have never seen before, and I am but one of them.' This is what he said to me.

"When the Zhaunagush came they brought the Horse with them. The People saw the Horse as special. They sought to learn its medicine. It became a sign of honour to ride these spirit beings, to race the wind with them. But the Zhaunagush could only see this act as thievery, as the behaviour of lesser people, so they called us horse thieves.

"The change that comes our way will come in many forms. In sights that are mysterious to our eyes, in sounds that are grating on our ears, in ways of thinking that will crash like thunder in our hearts and minds. But we must learn to ride each one of these horses of change. It is what the future asks of us and our survival depends on it. That is the spirit teaching of the Horse."

The People did not know what to make of this talk. Shabogeesick's words scared them. But they trusted him and they had come to love Kitchi-Animoosh. So they took good care of him, fed him choice grains and hay that they traded for at the rail line. The children rode him to keep him fit. When the treaty men found us in our isolated camp and made us sign our names to the register, they were surprised to see the horse. When they asked how he had come to be there, the People pointed at Shabogeesick, and it was the Zhaunagush who called him Indian Horse. It has been our family name ever since.

———— 3

All that I knew of Indian died in the winter of 1961, when I was eight years old.

My grandmother, Naomi, was very old then. She was the matriarch of the small band of people I was born to. We still lived a bush life at that time. We had little contact with anyone besides the Zhaunagush at the Northern Store in Minaki, where we took our furs and berries, or the odd group of wandering Indians who stumbled across our camps. If there was ever a sign of an approaching stranger, our grandmother hurried my brother Benjamin and me off into the bush. We would stay there until the stranger departed, even if that took a day or so.

There was a spectre in our camp. We could see the shadow of this dark being in the lines of our mother's face. She would sometimes sit huddled close to the fire, clenching and unclenching her fists, her eyes dark moons in the firelight. She never spoke at times like that, never could be comforted. I'd walk to her and take her hand but she didn't notice me. It was as if she was under the influence of a potent medicine no shaman had the power to break. The spectre lived in the other adults too, my father and my aunt and uncle. But its most chilling presence was in my mother.

"The school," she would whisper then. "The school."

It was the school that Naomi hid us from. It was the school that had turned my mother so far inward she sometimes ceased to exist in the outside world. Naomi had seen the adults of our camp taken away as children. She'd seen them return bearing a sorrow that could not be reached, and when my grandfather died, she took her family back to the land, hoping that an Ojibway life might heal them, ease their pain.

Besides my brother, I had a sister that I never met. Her name was Rachel, and the year before I was born she disappeared. She was six.

"The Zhaunagush came from across the water," our grandmother told Benjamin and me one time when we were hidden in the trees. "It was the end of August and we were coming back to the river from the summer camp near One Man Lake. Our canoes were full of berries. We planned to go to Minaki to sell them and buy supplies for the winter. We were tired.

"I never thought they'd come in the dawn. Me, I always thought the Zhaunagush slept late like fat old bears. But they walked into our camp and I pulled my robe up over Benjamin who was so small and hid him from their view. But they found Rachel and they took her away in their boat.

"I stood on the rocks and watched them. Them, they had a boat with a motor, and when they rounded the bend in the river I thought how fast things can vanish from our view. Her screams hung in the air like smoke from a green fire. But even they finally vanished and all that was left was the wake from that boat slapping at the rocks at my feet.

"That's all I carry of her now—the wet slap of water on the rocks. Every time I hear it I remember the dawn the white men came and stole Rachel from us."

So we hid from the white men. Benjamin and I developed the quick ears of bush people. When we detected the drone of an engine we knew to run. We'd grab the old lady's hand and scuttle into the trees and find a place to secret ourselves away until we knew for certain that there was no danger.

I learned English at the same time I learned Ojibway. My father taught me to read from Zhaunagush books, taught me to form the sounds the letters built with the tip of his finger as my guide. They felt hard, those white man words; sharp and pointed on my tongue. Old Naomi fought against it, trying to throw the books in the fire.

"They come in different ways, them, the Zhaunagush," she said. "Their talk and their stories can sneak you away as quick as their boats."

So I grew up afraid of the white man. As it turned out, I had reason to be.

In 1957, when I was four, they got my brother, Benjamin. The old lady and I were gathering roots in a glade back of the trees that stood against the river. The men and my brother were at the foot of a rapids setting gill nets. The airplane came out of the west, and we did not hear it soon enough. Naomi and I made it to a cleft in the rocks, but the men and my brother had nowhere to go. The plane cut them off, and we crawled up out of our crevice in the rocks and watched as those men from the plane lowered a canoe and forced my family's canoe to the opposite shore. They had guns, those Zhaunagush. I think that if they hadn't, my father and my uncle would have fought them off and we would have run into the back country. But they took my brother at gunpoint and pushed him up into the plane.

My mother collapsed on the long, flat rock that reached out into the river at our camp. No one could move her. She lay there for days, and it was only the chill of the first autumn rains that got her up on her feet and back to the fire. She was lost to me then. I could see that. She was gaunt and drained from days of weeping, a tent of skin over her bones. When Benjamin disappeared he carried a part of her away with him, and there was nothing anyone could do to fill it. My father tried. He never left her side for weeks. But now that she had lost two children, she would not speak anything except "the school," the words like a bruise in the air. So he left her—and he and my uncle paddled off downriver to sell the berries. When they returned they brought the white man with them in brown bottles. Spirits, Naomi called them. Bad spirits. Those spirits made the grown-ups move in strange, jerky ways and their talk was twisted. I fell asleep to evil laughter. Sometimes my mother lurched to her feet and danced around the fire, and the shadow she threw against the skin of the tent was like the outline of a skeleton. I clutched my robe tight to my throat, lay across the space my brother once filled and waited for sleep to claim me.

On clear nights the old woman and I would sit on the rocks by the edge of the river. The stars pinwheeled above us and we would hear wolves calling to each other. Naomi told me stories of the old days. Told me about my grandfather and the medicine ways he carried. Good medicine. Powerful, Ojibway medicine. The river wound serpentine, radiant in the light of the northern moon. In its curling wash I sometimes thought I could hear songs sung in Ojibway. Honour songs, raising me above the hurt of my brother's absence. That voice sustained me, as did the firm, warm hand of Naomi on the thin blade of my shoulder.

4 —————

After Benjamin disappeared my family left the bush and the shores of the river. We canoed out one day and left the camp behind. My grandmother came too though she'd argued against the move. My mother seemed almost weightless by now. I was always surprised that she left footprints. There was nothing to her but air. Her eyes were empty and she walked bent over like an old woman.

My father bore it all in stoic silence. But there was an angry arc when he swung an axe, a more vicious slice of the knife when he skinned out a deer. This energy, so heavy and thick, was the opposite of my mother's.

Both my parents had taken to the Zhaunagush drink, and we left the bush in pursuit of it. We followed the whiskey to the transient camps of the half-breeds who gathered on the discard lands around sawmill towns, waiting for the bits of work that were sometimes tossed their way. Indian work. That's what the mill folk called it. Men and boys would plow off into the bush to cut deadfall trees and haul their lengths to cleared stretches where the skidders could get to them. It was their job to clear the bastard trees that made dropping the prime timber more difficult for the white fallers. There were no chainsaws. The breeds and the

Indians cut everything by hand with Swede saws and axes. It was brutal work for little pay and what was paid out was drunk off quickly. There weren't many kids in those camps. Most of them had been spirited away by the government men. The fact that no one ever came for me was more a testament to the invisible nature of our lives than to any good luck. I hauled a wagon around the rutted, muddy roads that led through the tent village and out to the desolate edges of the town where the poor whites lived, to sell firewood we kids broke by hand. Broke-wood breeds. That's what the Zhaunagush at the mills called us. Broke-wood breeds.

Our lives became the plod from one tent village to another. Sometimes there'd be an abandoned tarpaper shack that we could call home, but for the most part we lived with others as displaced as we were, in canvas tents strung in a circle around a central fire. We'd share the warmth and whatever food we had. I learned to snare rabbits and steal chickens. I grew to hate the stink of sulfur at the same time I learned to endure the stench of roasted dog, the bite of the pine gum tea washing down the lard sandwiches that were our staple. Naomi told me stories, kept me away from the adults when they were in the grips of the drink. She showed me how to skin the squirrels and woodchucks we could sometimes catch in those thin woods.

We settled in at Redditt in the winter of 1960. There was a lot of work for the men there. We managed to buy a wood stove for our tent and passed the deep snow moons in a comfort we'd forgotten could exist. With this infusion of hope, my father drank less. There was more money for food, and I stopped snapping off the ends of the branches that stuck up out of the snow to haul about in my wagon. By spring I'd grown taller, elastic and wiry.

That spring we gathered mushrooms and greens and wild onions. A stream led from a bog lake to the main river, and my grandmother showed me how to lay out a burlap bag and haul in the suckers that ran up the creek to spawn. I learned to clean them with swift swipes of a knife and use the guts for bait on night lines I set out to drift in the current of the big river. We smoked those fish. Sometimes we'd slap thick coats of clay around them and bake them in the fire. My grandmother used the ribs of them for needles to sew buttons on my battered shirts. It began to feel as though we might forge a life for ourselves there on the edges of that rough-hewn town. Summer came. My mother sat with us at the fire most nights, even though she still carried such a deep sadness.

———— 5

Then Benjamin walked out of the bush. He'd run away from the school in Kenora. People he met told him where we'd gotten to, and he'd followed the rail line north, and then the road. It was sixty miles to Redditt and he'd walked all that way. He was bug-bit and thin, taller than when we'd last seen him. His hair was cropped close to his skin and his ill-fitting clothes were made even looser by the weight he'd lost on his journey. For a moment no one knew who he was.

"Mother," he said.

My mother burst out of her despair in a gale of tears and laughter.

There was great celebration. My brother sat by the fire and was fed our thin stew and my grandmother mixed up bannock that she baked on a stick over the fire. I stood by his side while he chewed. He was different. Not only in size. There was a wariness in his eyes and a hardness to the set of his chin. His hands shook some when he tore off bits of the bannock. "Saul," he'd greeted me, nodding firmly. It was odd to see the expressions of a grown man on a boy's face. Then he coughed.

The cough racked him, and he bent forward. The hump of his back rose and fell with the effort. The grown-ups shrank back a step, fear on their faces. Only my grandmother stepped up to attend to him. She leaned him back against her bosom and cradled his head. His coughs subsided gradually. When they left him finally, his face was red and there were tears in his eyes. I could see how much smaller the spell had made him. He huddled close to my grandmother and put a hand to his mouth and worked at breathing regularly. "The coughing sick," she said to us. "He got it from the school."

Over the next few days my brother rested. It would be years before I knew the full name of what he had but the TB my brother carried in his lungs spread anxiety throughout my family. My mother retreated into her woe again. My father drank hard. One evening my grandmother coaxed everyone to the fire and spoke to us.

"There is not much time," she said. "The coughing sick is in Benjamin hard, and I think that soon the Zhaunagush will come to find him. When they do, they will find Saul and we will lose them both."

We needed to go where the government men could not find us, my grandmother said. We needed to get back to living in a proper way. We needed to take Benjamin to a place where the air and the land could ease his spirit.

"He is twelve," she said. "Saul is seven. They are old enough now to dance the *manoomin,* the rice, in the old way. Their grandfather would have wanted this for them. We will go to Gods Lake."

No one argued. In the firm words of the old woman there was no room for discussion. We began to prepare for the trip. My father used his last paycheque to buy three old freighter canoes that he and my uncle and grandmother patched with spruce gum heated over the fire. The old lady quietly traded my father's whiskey for a rifle and shells and a pair of heavy metal washtubs. We packed our tents and what food we could and set off to paddle our way to where Gods Lake sat in the thickest part of the bush country. Grandmother knew the country and she guided us through the portages to the Winnipeg River, then north past Minaki, then east again beyond One Man Lake. The journey took us ten days. Benjamin and I sat in the middle of one of the large canoes with our grandmother in the stern, directing us past shoals and through rapids and into magnificent stretches of water. One day the clouds hung low and light rain freckled the slate-grey water that peeled across our bow. The pellets of rain were warm and Benjamin and I caught them on our tongues as our grandmother laughed behind us. Our canoes skimmed along and as I watched the shoreline it seemed the land itself was in motion. The rocks lay lodged like hymns in the breast of it, and the trees bent upward in praise like crooked fingers. It was glorious. Ben felt it too. He looked at me with tears in his eyes, and I held his look a long time, drinking in the face of my brother. When he coughed I put a hand to his back.

"In the Long Ago Time before the Zhaunagush, a group of hunters set out to find moose late one fall." My grandmother's voice carried over the water, and the other two canoes pulled even with us so the adults could hear. "They went the way we go now, and they'd never seen such strength in the country. The rocks seemed to sing to them.

"In those times our people relied on intuition—the great spirit strength of thought—and the hunters found a portage at a flat place not far from where we are now. It led back into country marked with ridges. It was very hard to walk, but they followed a small creek through a cut in the land until they felt the land close off behind them like the flap of a wigwam. They could feel the stillness in their bones, and some of them were afraid. But the need for meat for the coming winter was so strong they pushed on.

"Finally the creek led them to a hidden lake. The shoreline was narrow and the curve of the lake's bowl was steep, except for one section that sloped upward gradually out of a tamarack bog. The hunters knew there would be moose there and they were heartened. They began exploring to find the place where it would be easiest to dress their game. The water of that lake was black and still, though, and the silence that hung over it made them nervous. The hunters had the feeling of being watched from the trees.

"Finally the men came to a spot where a cliff spilled gravel downward to form a wide beach. There were shallows for landing their canoes near a good stand of trees and thickets of willow. It seemed a perfect place to make their camp. They beached the canoes and stood on that gravel shore and looked around them. The air did not move. It felt hard to draw a breath, and their feeling of being watched was stronger.

"As they started to unload, the hunters heard laughter from the trees and the low roll of voices speaking in the Old Talk, the original language, unspoken but for ceremony. But no one was there. As they splashed through the shallows in a panic trying to get their canoes back into the water, laughter rolled openly from the trees. The hairs on the back of those hunters' necks stood straight up, and they trembled as they paddled back to the head of the portage. By the time they made it back to their home, every hair on their heads was white.

"The people called the place *Manitou Gameeng,* and it became Gods Lake when the Zhaunagush missionaries heard the tale. No one could stay there; whenever anybody tried, a powerful presence would overwhelm them and they would run away. But Solomon had a dream. In that dream our family were harvesting rice at Gods Lake and we were content and settled and the sky was a deep and cloudless blue. So we went there one spring. We made a ceremony on the rocks at the base of that cliff and we sang old songs and said prayers in the Old Talk and prepared a feast and carried Spirit Plates into the trees and left them there. We made a sacred fire and we burned the last of the food and your grandfather climbed high up the face of that cliff and laid a tobacco offering there.

"The air thinned and the breeze began to blow and there was peace. But no one else has been able to go there since. They are still chased away. Only the Indian Horse family can go to Gods Lake. It is our territory. The rice that grows at the southern end is ours to harvest, and we will gather it in the traditional way as another offering to the Old Ones."

The story spooked us. Even the adults, who had heard it many times before, grew silent. I wondered what would become of us there. I wondered if the spirit, the *manitous,* of Gods Lake would look upon us with pity and compassion, if we would flourish on this land that was ours alone.

6 ⎯⎯⎯⎯

We made Gods Lake in the early afternoon of a day in late summer. It was a great bowl of inkpot black sunk into the granite and edged with spruce, pine and fir. At its shoreline, as my grandmother had told us, were tall cedars, a tamarack bog and a wide shallow bay at the southern end, where manoomin grew in abundance. The air was still at first. But as we paddled toward the northern end, where the grey-white cliffs spilled their gravel down to form the beach, a breeze came up and we could hear bird sounds from the reeds and shallows. A pair of eagles watched us from the top of a ragged old pine. A mother bear and two cubs broke apart at our approach and galloped up through the bracken and the meadow to disappear into the trees at its edge. It was warm and the sky above us was festooned with small clouds.

We pitched our tents in a glade in the trees. Every morning I could flip back the flap of the tent my brother and I shared and see the water and the opposite shore, the mist off it dreamlike. There were game and fish and berries and we ate like we never had before. Everyone seemed to take to the promise of this place. Ben rallied enough to help me with gathering firewood, setting the night lines and tramping up to the top of the ridge where we would sit and just look out over the land. The gods of Gods Lake seemed pleased that we were there, and as the weeks dwindled off to the far edge of summer, our camp was light-hearted and peaceful.

I tramped up the ridge alone as my brother slept in the tent late one afternoon. From there it seemed as though the entire world was a carpet of green pocked with bald grey places where spires and shoulders of rock rose through the trees. The sky was a clear and endless blue. A faint breeze eased over the lake. I'd come to favour a small jut of pink granite that looked like the bottom of an over-turned canoe. From it I could see in every direction, and I loved being surrounded by all of that amazing space. As I sat there with the warmth of the sun spilled over me, I closed my eyes. I could hear the breeze in the trees. There was a tempo to it. Slow. Measured. My breathing slowed to match it. That's when I heard my name. It was whispered so softly, I thought at first that I'd imagined it. Then I heard it again. My eyes flew open and I looked around. No one was there, only the branches of the trees bouncing easily in the breeze. Frail clouds had fanned out across the great canopy of blue sky. I stood and walked to the edge of the ridge and looked down. The drop was steep.

"Saul." It came to me long and stretched out so that it didn't really sound like a word at all. But I heard it none-theless. "Saul."

When I looked down at the lake again, I saw people. They were busy in canoes setting nets. A group of women waded in the shallows gathering cattail roots, and laughing children splashed at minnows. A few young men walked out of the trees carrying deer carcasses on poles, and now I could see a camp of a dozen wigwams at the foot of the great cliff. Women were scraping hides stretched out on poplar frames while children ran around them. A pair of elders sat beside a fire, and as I watched, one of the men looked up at me and nodded. He raised his black bowl pipe in my direction.

Then, suddenly, it was night. The fire at the centre of the camp burned high and in the flickering light I could see people dancing. Someone played a hand drum and the song they sang pierced the darkness where I stood with high, jubilant syllables of praise. The fire sent the fragrances of cedar and sage and roasting meat up to me and I felt a great hunger. The moon was full in the sky. As the rhythm of the drum and the song slowed, it became a social dance and I heard laughter clear as the call of night birds.

Then it was the deep of night and in the dim blue light of that full moon the camp slept. The fire had dwindled to lazy smoke curling up and over everything. A pair of dogs slept close to it. At the foot of the rock beach, canoes bumped and jostled in the light push of wavelets breaking on the stone. The man I had seen earlier by the fire was standing on the beach and he was singing. He held a long stick with a glowing end, and I could smell sweetgrass, tobacco, cedar and sage as he set the stick down on a flat rock and fanned the smoke up and over himself with a long feather fan. In the song that rose up to me I heard fragments of the Old Talk. The man raised his arms up high with his fingers splayed. When he'd finished singing, he bowed his head. Silence lay heavy over everything. I shivered. A long time passed, and then out of the west came the wail of a wolf song. The wolf song rose higher and higher and as it reached its crescendo I saw the face of the old man in the face of the moon. He stared back at me and the light in his eyes comforted me. Then he closed his eyes slowly and everything changed again.

Now it was morning. The fog rising up off the lake moved across the rock beach to envelop the camp. A rumble shook the ground at my feet and I heard the sound of rock cascading.

I fell to the ground as the rumbling grew louder. A cloud of dust rolled over me. When the rumble had subsided, the silence was so deep it scared me. I crept to the edge of the ridge and looked over. The face of the cliff had collapsed, and the camp was gone. Vanished. Even the trees had been scraped away and the beach was strewn with boulders. The chalky smell of rock dust brought tears to my eyes and I stood there weeping, my shoulders shaking at the thought of those people buried under all that stone.

"Saul," I heard behind me.

I turned and my grandmother was standing there with her arms spread open. I fell into them and cried into her bosom.

My grandmother never explained it, but there really was no need. I knew now why Gods Lake belonged to our family: because part of our family had died there, and their spirits still spoke from the trees. Somehow, knowing that was a comfort to me.

Ben and I learned from the women how to fashion elaborate braids out of red willow bark. There was a design to the weave, and grandmother watched us to make sure we made them correctly.

"Before the changes the Zhaunagush brought, the people would make *mamaawash-kawipidoon,* rice ties just like these. Each family had their own braid tied their special way so that they could be recognized in the rice beds. Each head of rice is tied with these." She talked as she worked. It was as though her hands could think on their own. "We make a ceremony out of the gathering. It teaches us to remember that rice is a gift of Creator."

"It is a gift from God," my aunt said quietly.

The old woman replied slowly. "No matter how you make the address, the sender remains the same."

"We should pray with the rosary and give thanks the proper way," my aunt said. "This way is wrong."

"Blasphemy," my mother agreed.

"That school gave you words that do not apply to us," my grandmother said. "Out here there is no need to keep the spirit bound to fear."

"We were taught to be God-fearing," my mother said.

"One who loves does not brandish fear or require it." The old woman stopped her braiding to look at my mother and aunt, but they kept their heads down and continued with the ties. "Here in this old way you may rediscover that and reclaim it as your own."

I didn't understand the words they spoke that day. I only knew that it felt right and good to do the chore we did, the simple ceremony of making rice ties. When we were finished, my grandmother and Ben and I paddled out in a canoe and she showed us how to tie the heads of the rice so it could be harvested more efficiently. She used a long, forked pole to push us around the rice beds. In the slow, steady motion of the canoe, my brother and I followed our grandmother's directions. I didn't realize until later, when the tent flaps were down and I could hear the voices of the adults over the snap of the fire, that my brother had not coughed the entire time. He slept quietly that whole night.

WHEN THE RICE MOON came, Ben and I were put in charge of digging a pair of shallow firepits and gathering firewood. Then we dug another, larger, slightly deeper pit a few yards away from the fires and lined it with a canvas tarpaulin. On the day of the harvest we started the fires early in the morning. In the dawn chill my grandmother sang in the Old Talk, her voice reverberating off the water and echoing back from the face of the cliff. She sprinkled fresh cedar on that fire. My brother and I hauled the crisp air deep into us and tried to join in the old woman's song even though we did not know the words. Ben coughed and had to stop. My parents and my aunt and uncle hung back near the trees, the toe of my father's boot tracing circles in the dirt.

After we'd eaten, the adults paddled off to the rice beds. Ben and I tended the fire and when there was a good bed of embers we propped the metal wash basins my grandmother had brought across stout green logs to heat them. We knew what would go on in the canoes. She'd told us.

"The men will pole the canoes through the stocks. We women will pull the heads of the rice down with a stick. Then we'll knock that stick with a swing of another one and the rice will fall into the canoe."

The solid clap of sticks travelled back across the water.

"We keep on knocking that rice until the canoes can't hold any more. Then the men will guide us back here to the fires."

We heard a shout after about an hour. In the distance the canoes emerged from the rice beds, so low in the water I thought they would sink. The women were sitting on the bottom. We could see the rice piled up over their legs, which they'd covered with thick pants to ward off the bite of the rice worms. My grandmother and mother and aunt paddled lightly. The men stood at the sterns and used the tip of their paddles to ease the canoes forward. It seemed to take them forever to travel the breadth of the lake. When they got closer I waded into the water to help pull the bows of the canoes as close to the beach as they would go. I helped the women out and the four of us hauled the canoes up onto the stone shore. Once my father and uncle had hauled the canoes out of the water, we began throwing rice into the metal washtubs.

When the tubs were filled the men carried them to the fire and the women took the canoe paddles and sifted the rice. The smoke curled up and around them and they rubbed at their eyes. As they worked, my father and uncle walked into the bush and returned with two long poles that they stripped of bark and propped up in holes they'd dug at the sides of the deeper, canvas-lined pit. When the rice had parched sufficiently over the heat, my grandmother signalled for Ben and me to take up our positions beside the men.

"In the old days, it was important for boys to learn to be men, to be responsible. This dancing of the rice was one of the first ways they did that," my grandmother said.

"Rice is sacred. When Creator sent the Anishinabeg, the Ojibway, east from the Big Water to find their homeland, we were instructed to stop when we came to the place where food grew on the water. This country of rice was the place we found.

"You boys will crush the hulls of the parched rice from the seed with careful, steady steps. I will use your grandfather's rattle as I sing the ricing song. The poles beside the pit will help you keep your balance."

Our grandmother came to smudge our feet with the sacred herbs and mumble a prayer. When she took up the rattle and began to sing, Ben and I stepped into the pit. The rice pods shifted crazily under our feet and we struggled to keep time with the song. The dried seeds in the rattle sounded like hulls of rice. The crunch of the pods beneath our feet took on a beat that we struggled to maintain. When she had determined that the batch was hulled, our grandmother signalled us to stop.

After Ben and I climbed out of the pit, my father and uncle lifted the tarpaulin and poured the rice out on a blanket set on the rocks near the shore. My mother and aunt loaded flat baskets with rice, turned to face the breeze and began flipping the rice into the air. I watched as the breeze caught the rice and blew the crushed hulls away. Then the pit was loaded again and Benjamin and I began to tread the fresh batch. We worked that way all morning, legs burning. Benjamin tried to hide his coughing from the adults. I wanted to call out, but he looked at me with his fist held to his mouth and shook his head.

The sun was high when we stepped into the pit for the last of the load. My brother splashed himself with water and wiped at his face. He leaned harder on the pole, doubling over with coughs that shook him mightily. He managed only a few strides before the coughs hit him again. A spume of blood flew out of his mouth and sprinkled the rice at our feet. Benjamin leaned on the pole and fell onto his side on the edge of the pit. I yelled.

We dragged my brother from the pit and laid him on a blanket in the trees. He couldn't stop coughing and his lungs made a wet, slushy sound. Finally my grandmother said we should move him.

My brother was limp and hot and he felt thin in my hands. Empty. When we laid him on the spruce boughs in the tent he seemed to sink into them, as though the land were already reaching out and claiming him.

We took turns bringing him water, the old woman and I. The others stayed away. We could hear them talking by the fire, but my grandmother was too busy making teas and potions, using roots she'd found by searching the nearby bush, to pay them any mind. I could feel the chasm between the three of us and the others as if it were a living thing. There seemed no way to cross that distance. It was the first time I recall being afraid of my parents. They stoked the fire and sat in its shadow. The moon rose. When I couldn't keep my eyes open any longer, I leaned against my grandmother outside the tent where my brother hacked in the darkness, and fell asleep.

He was dead by morning.

8 ———

My mother's keening by the river was eerie. My father stood at the fire rubbing his hands together and mumbling to himself. My aunt and uncle sat with their arms around each other while she said the rosary and wept. It was my grandmother who prepared my brother's body. She took water from the lake, dipped cedar boughs in it and washed him. I could hear her singing in the tent. The tightness in my throat almost made me cough too. No one came to ask me how I was. Instead, when the old woman finished with her ministrations, she came out of the tent and called us all to the fire.

"We will honour him in the old way," she said. "We will carry him to a high point and lay him in the breast of the earth with his feet pointed east facing the morning sun. That way his spirit can follow the sun as it makes its journey across the sky and begin his Spirit Walk."

"Heathen," my mother spat. "He is my son. We will take him to the priest."

"They will not honour him."

"You do not honour him," my mother cried. "You brought him to this forsaken place. You told us by coming here that we would return to how things were. But those ways are gone. Those gods are dead. We need to take my son to the priest so that he can be returned to the bosom of Christ."

"Your grief has blinded you." My grandmother held out the bowl that contained the sacred medicines but my mother slapped it away.

"You have no say. He is my son. He will have the rites of the Church. We'll take this rice that cost him his life and we'll sell it and buy him a coffin and he will have a proper burial. Not out here. Not stuck in some hole in the earth."

My mother walked to my father and took his hand and led him away from the fire. My aunt and uncle followed. We could see them all talking by the water. My father came back alone and stood across the fire from the old lady.

"We'll take him to the priest now," he said. "There's a lot of the day left and we can get a good start."

"You know what your father would have said?" she asked.

"No," he said. "I have not heard his voice in a long time."

"He would have said that all gods are one."

"She won't hear that."

"Do you?"

My father pinched his lips together and rocked on the balls of his feet. I could sense the struggle in him. "*Kaween.* No. I guess I don't," he said. "She said to tell you that you could either come with us or not."

"I won't come."

"We'll be gone a spell. Can you look after Saul? Better he waits here with you."

"He'll be fine with me. There's food. We have snares and the net."

"All right, then."

"All right."

The adults packed two canoes with the bags of rice. They left a small sack for us. They gathered their clothes and other food for the journey, and when they were ready to leave they came to the fire. At that moment my parents seemed like strangers to me. Maybe it was the grief over my brother's death that made them move so deliberately. Sometimes I think that if I had yelled something it would have all been different. But no words were in me. I watched my uncle and my father carry my brother's body from the tent wrapped in a blanket and lug it to the canoe. They set him in the middle, leaned back against sacks of rice. I cried. I wept harder than I ever had. I wanted to stop this, wanted to bring them all back beside the fire and hear my grandmother's guiding voice telling us stories and showing us the direction we should go together. As they eased the canoes out into the shallows, my grandmother pulled me close to her and put a hand on my head.

Even now when I think back to that day, I can see the shimmer of the wake they left behind them, the vee of it and the divergent lines that lapped at the shoreline. I can still see the bent back of my father paddling, the slumped form of my mother in the bow waving at the water with her oar. I can see the canoe that held my brother's body as it passed the rock cairn and slid out of my view forever.

—— 9

The adults didn't come back. When the autumn began to turn I could tell the old woman was worried. That terrified me. The sky turned to the pale, washed-out blue of late October. Geese were in flight and my grandmother used some of the shells to bring down a few. We plucked them and slow roasted them over a green wood fire along with the fish I'd gill netted. She showed me how to use moss and thin strips of sod from beneath the trees to line the edges of our tent, and then we padded the floor extra thick with spruce boughs against the frost. As the nights became colder, ice appeared at the edge of the water. I set snares in the woods but they came up empty. We woke to snow one morning. The old woman walked off into the trees alone with her pipe and her rattle. I could hear her singing and praying. I sat by the fire and waited, and her keening echoed back from across the water as though others were with her in the trees. She came back and sat beside me and we drank tea.

"We can't wait for them," she said.

"What will we do?"

"We have to take the canoe and go down river to Minaki. My brother's son Minoose lives there. We can stay with him through the winter if we have to."

"Where did they go?" I asked.

She set her cup on the log and took out her pipe and loaded it and sat and smoked and stared at the fire. "I don't know," she said, finally. "I asked the grandfathers and the grandmothers for vision, but they have moved beyond the reach of the Old Ones now."

"Will we find them?"

"I don't know. But here we will die."

—————— 10

Keewatin. That's the name of the north wind. The Old Ones gave it a name because they believed it was alive, a being like all things. Keewatin rises out over the edge of the barren lands and grips the world in fierce fingers born in the frigid womb of the northern pole. The world slows its rhythm gradually, so that the bears and the other hibernating creatures notice time's relentless prowl forward. But the cold that year came fast. It descended on us like a slap of a hand: sudden and vindictive.

We loaded the canoe with the last of the geese and the fish. We were freezing. The old woman made me pile on clothing and she cut shawls for us out of the canvas of a tent. She'd made boots for us out of the same cloth and we tied them to our feet with rope around our ankles. It was snowing. The pellets were like comets whirring in from space. I remember thinking I could hear them. It took all we had to cross the lake to the portage. The old woman's face was strained with the effort of paddling into the teeth of that wind. The whitecaps slapped up at our hands. But we made it, and when we hauled the canoe up and into the shelter of the trees, the absence of wind made it feel like we were stepping into a dwelling.

"We'll have to walk the supplies out first," she said. She took our canvas shawls and fashioned them into sacks and we piled everything into them and slung them on our backs. The walk along the creek was hard. Frost covered the rocks and we slipped often. The air froze our hands into claws where we gripped the rope that bound the canvas. We had to breathe through our mouths because the ice crystals froze our nostrils together. When we reached the shore of the river the old woman took my hands and put them up her skirt and held them between her thighs to warm them. I wasn't embarrassed. I put my face against her belly, and when we had rested we walked back to the canoe. She made a harness out of rope and I walked the front of it while she hoisted the stern with a stick of alder, and together we slumped up the length of that creek and got that long canoe up the portage. It taxed us completely. She turned the boat over and we lay beneath it with the canvas slung over us and the snow hissing through the air outside. When I woke she had a fire going and I could smell goose fat and strong tea. We ate without speaking and my grandmother kept her eyes on the river. The water was black with the cold. We edged the canoe closer to the fire and tilted it and she put spruce boughs on the ground and over the hull to form a lean-to, and that's where we slept that first night. We could hear wolves and the snapping of branches in the trees and she pulled me closer. The land around us was like a great being hunched in the darkness. In the morning there was an inch or more of snow and we had a breakfast of cold fish and tea. Then we set the canoe to the water and pushed off west to where the river swung south and then east again toward the railroad town of Minaki.

She sang while we paddled. Her songs sounded like prayers. I hoped they were. The cold was intense. Mist came off the water and everything was grey with the frost. The only sound was the peeling of the water across our bow. The humped shapes of boulders on the shore wore cloaks of white. Trees with new snow heavy in their branches looked like tired soldiers heading home from war. The glisten of ice. When my hands became too cold to paddle I put them in my armpits to warm them and the old lady paddled us forward. The snow began again in mid-afternoon.

It was falling straight down and spinning, plummeting, the wind dying off. Snow piled up in the belly of the boat. When the snow became too dense to see, the old lady eased us to shore between a pair of stones the size of wigwams.

The cold was an awesome beast. As I plowed through the knee-deep snow to forage firewood I could feel the beast tracking me, waiting for the exhaustion to fell me so it could feed on my frozen flesh. The fire we built against it was tiny. The wood hissed and I feared the flames would wink out. But the old woman humped off into the bush and came back with arms filled with fir branches, and when she threw them on the fire it blazed high and hot and crackling. Snow fell like pieces of stars through the night.

We ran out of food on the third day. By then the water was too cold to swallow. I could feel my teeth crack when I tried. My grandmother cut a swatch of buckskin from her moccasin and told me to suck on it like a soother. It tasted like moss, but it offered a little moisture. At a bend in the river we came across a deer standing at the shore. The old woman raised her rifle but she was shivering too much to aim. The buck raised its nose and watched us. That night she fed me a soup of spruce gum, berries dug from the snow, moss and stones.

Both of us dozed off in the canoe that fourth day. The river sent us shooting into a gap strewn with boulders and we woke with a shock when we hit one full on. The belly of the boat split at the nose and water poured in. We scrambled over its side into water thigh deep. My grandmother grabbed my hand and we pushed on toward shore. The water felt like knives of cold steel. When we made shore we turned and watched the canoe spin lazily in the current and then drift away, the bob of the last of our supplies heartbreaking.

The snow was even deeper now. The old lady waded through it, tugging me into a thick copse of cedars. She tore branches from them and piled them on the snow and made me lie down in them. She took off her canvas shawl, laid it over me and covered me with more cedar boughs. When I closed my eyes the dark was luxurious and I turned to it and let the sleep come. I felt slow and lifted on billows of air. Drifting. In my mind I saw the shores of Gods Lake as it was in the late summer. The sky was high and cloudless and easing toward sunset. I was drifting in the canoe a hundred yards from shore, and there were the shadows of my family, my people, dancing around a fire, and there was singing and the sound of a drum and the vague stir of laughter from the trees. I was weightless, boneless and very, very tired. The old woman slapped me awake.

"Gods in the trees," I said, dreamily. My voice seemed to come from far away.

She slapped me again and I came to in the bracing push of the freeze. She'd cut sod and trundled it back. Together we gathered branches and made a small domed frame above the boughs on the snow, then covered it with the rest of the cedar and the sod patches. It wasn't very big but there was enough room for us to crawl in and pull the canvas shawls over us. Our body heat kept us warm.

That night I fell asleep to my grandmother's voice. She told me stories of the Star People who had come to our people in the Long Ago Time and brought teachings, secrets of the cosmos and the basis of our spiritual way. When I woke halfway through the night she was still talking, but her voice was weaker. The old story took me off into sleep again. When morning came she looked tired. Worn away. We were hungry. We stood shivering in the snow. She followed the shore of the river with her eyes.

"There was a trail your great-grandfather cut that led from those rapids through the bush to the railroad tracks south of here," she said. "Can you see it?"

I squinted at the impenetrable wall of trees. There was nothing to indicate a trail. But I closed my eyes. I could hear the hiss of the river coursing past the rocks. I hauled in a deep lungful of air and raised my head. I felt snowflakes land on my upturned face.

"Saul," I heard from the trees.

When I opened my eyes, I could see a slight bellying in the snow. It arced southward to a break in the trees so slight it was nearly invisible. "There," I said.

We plowed through the knee-deep snow around the marshes that bled into the river. The roofs of beaver houses showed far back in the reeds. We walked all that morning. My grandmother stopped every now and then to lean against a tree and catch her breath. I could see how old she was. Her skin looked pasted to her bones, made so leathery by the deep freeze that it looked as though it might snap off in chunks.

"Over that next ridge," I said and pointed. "There's a long gap that leads around a beaver lodge lake. The railroad tracks are on the other side."

"You can see it?" she asked.

"Yes," I said. She clutched my arm.

The sun was square in the sky when we made the foot of the ridge. My grandmother drew me close and pulled her canvas shawl over me. My feet were blocks of ice. The rope that held my canvas boots on had broken, so she took the rope fastening hers and tied them back around my ankles. Then she dug through the snow for clumps of moss to tie around my hands as mittens.

"What about you?" I asked.

"Got my gumption to keep me warm," she said. "We have to keep moving."

We made the railroad tracks within an hour or so. By then the wind had shifted and picked up intensity. It blew snow right into our faces. It drifted up between the ties. Lifting my legs over the ties was hard work, and at one point I fell over and lay there, too tired to get up. I felt her lift me. My eyes were heavy and my skin burned. I felt her stumble as she carried me, and I could hear her wheezing with the effort. I don't know how long we walked that way. After a while her steps grew shorter and she weaved. Then she fell too. When I opened my eyes I could see slats of painted wood behind her. We were on the platform of the railroad depot at Minaki. All around us was whirling snow and the white expanse where the tracks ran west to Manitoba and east into the frozen heart of the bush.

"We'll rest a minute," she wheezed. "Then we'll find Minoose."

I tucked my head in against her chest. She held me and we lay there in the darkness shivering. I could feel her tremble. Wrapped in the cracked canvas of an old tent, I huddled in the arms of the old woman and felt the cold freeze her in place. I understood that she had left me and I lay there crying against the empty drum of her chest.

After a while I heard shouts and the clump of feet. The wind bit into my face as the canvas shawl was pulled away.

"Jesus. There's a kid here."

Somebody lifted me up and I felt the old woman's arms fall away. I reached out to her, shouting in a mixture of Ojibway and English. She stayed slumped in the corner, her hair coated with snow. Her hands were cupped as though she was still holding on to me. I wanted to pull her to her feet so we could keep on walking. But instead I was borne away. A car door opened and I was lifted inside and set on the seat with a blanket thrown over me. The heat and the exhaustion pulled me under in a hot, red current.

If our canoe hadn't hit that boulder we would have made it to Minaki. We would have found Minoose and sheltered there, and my grandmother would have found a way to keep me with her. Instead, she was gone. Frozen to death saving me, and I was cast adrift on a strange new river.

11 ————

They took me to St. Jerome's Indian Residential School. I
read once that there are holes in the universe that swallow all light, all bodies. St. Jerome's took all the light from
my world. Everything I knew vanished behind me with an
audible swish, like the sound a moose makes disappearing
into spruce. We'd driven two days to get there. Two nuns
and three of us kids crammed into the back seat of a battered old Chev. A little girl who cried most of the way, and
another boy. We spent the trip without talking, taking
turns at the window watching the land flow by. It seemed
boundless. Every curve in that road, every crest of a hill,
even the cut of the trees against the night sky held me
spellbound. I barely slept.

I was lonely for the sky, for the feel of it on my face.

The school was a four-storey red brick building with
a cupola bearing a tall white cross as its only adornment.
There were no trees around it, only ground shrubs. A
wagon wheel leaned against a rock beside the large wooden
sign that read *St. Jerome's Indian Residential School.* A gravel
driveway curved toward the front entrance of wide concrete stairs with white-washed balustrades and double

doors of frosted glass. Two wings of the building thrust back behind. Beyond were sheds and barns and fields speckled with the rubble of furrows poking up through the thin snow. The entire property sat in a clearing at the top of a ridge with bush at its edges.

Inside, the smell of bleach and disinfectant, so strong it seemed to peel the skin off the inside of my nose. The floors were hardwood, sallow from decades of mopping and scrubbing. The walls were a sickly green. At every landing were doors of frosted glass so the light was pale and gave off a feeling of cold even though the radiators pulsed heat outward in waves. The linoleum on the steps was cracked in places but scrubbed to a dull sheen.

The fourth floor was one big room with windows at each side. Between them was a sea of cots, all folded and tucked in exactly the same manner. Regimented, though I didn't learn that word until much later.

The other boy and I were marched by a gruff priest to the back of this dormitory and ordered to strip and climb into tubs of nearly scalding water. After a minute the priest made us stand and threw handfuls of delousing powder over us. It bit at the corners of my eyes as he sat us in the tubs again to rinse it off. Then a pair of nuns scrubbed us with stiff-bristled brushes. The soap was harsh. They rubbed us nearly raw. It felt like they were trying to remove more than grime or odour. It felt as though they were trying to remove our skin. When it was over they handed us clothing and watched us while we dressed. The wool pants scratched at my skin. They were a size too big and had to be held up with a belt cinched tight. The shirt was stiff and white. The shoes were thin leather with laces and smooth, slippery soles. They made us walk awkwardly. Next, we sat in chairs with towels around our shoulders while the nuns shaved our hair down to nubby crew-cuts with electric clippers. I watched my long, straight hair land on the floor, and when I looked at the other boy he was crying. Huge, silent tears.

Back downstairs, we were made to stand in front of a desk in an office with windows looking out over the fields. We stood there a long time. Then the door opened and a priest and a large, reddish-faced nun stepped in.

"I'm Father Quinney and this is Sister Ignacia," the priest said. "This is our school. Well, more properly, it's the Lord's school, but he's put us in charge."

"Saul," Sister Ignacia said. "That's a fine biblical name. We won't need to change that. But we're going to have to do something about Lonnie Rabbit. I think Aaron is more suitable. From now on you are Aaron Rabbit. Do you understand?"

"But Lonnie is my dad's name," the boy said.

"Well, the Lord God is your father now and he wants you called Aaron."

"But I got a father."

Sister Ignacia strode out from behind the desk to stand directly in front of Lonnie, who looked down at the floor. "Your father is the Heavenly Father. You will learn that here. Your human father has nothing to offer you anymore."

"He's a trapper."

"He's a heathen."

"He's Ojibway."

"He is unbaptized and impure of spirit. When you use the word *father* at this school, it is your Heavenly Father you make reference to."

"I don't want no other father."

"You have no choice."

"I'll run."

The Sister smiled. It was chilling because there was no laughter in her eyes. They were a cold, pale blue, like the eyes of a husky, and when she reached behind her and brought a leather paddle into view she had a terrible calm about her. The paddle was blunt and wide and drilled with holes across its face. She cradled it in both palms, and with a blur of motion she twisted Lonnie around by the collar and pushed him to his knees. He screamed as the paddle struck his back. The nun yanked him to his feet as though he were a rag toy and struck him repeatedly behind the knees and on the back of the thighs. It sounded like she was beating a hide. Lonnie squirmed and struggled but her grip was incredible. She kept hitting him until he collapsed. Father Quinney stood with his hands behind his back and watched.

"Obedience is the measure of our worthiness." She spun Lonnie around to face her. "Here you will learn to be worthy. Do you hear me?"

"Yes," Lonnie said.

"Yes, Sister."

"Yes, Sister."

"That's a good boy." She reached out to lay a hand on his face. He flinched. She smiled again with the same ghastly lack of feeling. "At St. Jerome's we work to remove the

Indian from our children so that the blessings of the Lord may be evidenced upon them."

"Industry, boys," Father Quinney said. "Good, honest work and earnest study. That's what you'll do here. That's what will prepare you for the world."

Sister Ignacia took us each by a hand and, with a firm nod to the priest, led us from the office and out into the school. Her hands like dried birch bark. Her face composed, the slight press of a grin at the edges of her mouth. Beatific. That's another word I learned much later. As the Sister walked us through the school that first day, she had that saintly look on her face. The whistle of the leather still hung in the air. She was a large woman, tall, and I'd never known such terror.

In what seemed like an instant, the world I had known was replaced by an ominous black cloud.

———— 12

At St. Germ's the kids called me "Zhaunagush" because I could speak and read English. Most of them had been pulled from the deep North and knew only Ojibway. Speaking a word in that language could get you beaten or banished to the box in the basement the older ones had come to call the Iron Sister. There was no tolerance for Indian talk. On the second day I was there, a boy named Curtis White Fox had his mouth washed out with lye soap for speaking Ojibway. He choked on it and died right there in the classroom. He was ten. So the kids whispered to each other. They learned to speak without moving their lips, an odd ventriloquism that allowed them to keep their talk alive. They'd bend their heads close together as they mopped the halls or mucked out the barn stalls and speak Ojibway. I learned that ventriloquism eventually, but in the beginning they saw me as an outsider.

I didn't mind that. I was sore inside. The tearing away of the bush and my people was like ripped flesh in my belly. Every time I moved or was forced to speak, it roared its incredible pain. And so I took to isolation. I wasn't a large boy and I could disappear easily. I learned that I could draw the boundaries of my physical self inward, collapse the space I occupied and become a mote, a speck, an indifferent atom in its own peculiar orbit. Maybe it was the hurt itself that allowed me that odd grace. Maybe it was the memory of my grandmother's frozen arms around me or that last glimpse of my parents disappearing into the portage at Gods Lake. I don't know. But in my chrysalis of silence I turned to Zhaunagush books and language, finding in them a path beyond the astringent smell of the school. The nuns and the priests took me for studious and encouraged me to vanish even further into my self-imposed exile. It was easy.

You couldn't be a kid under that regime. There was no room for any kind of creativity to flourish. Instead, to survive, we mimicked the cloister walk of the nuns, a relentless mute march from prayer to chapel to physical labour.

Arden Little Light was a skinny Oji-Cree kid with a bad limp from where a trap had sprung closed on his ankle. His family lived so far back in the bush they couldn't get him out to a hospital. So the break in his bone had healed all ragged and calcified, leaving a ring beneath his skin like the bumps on a sturgeon's back. He always had a runny nose and he wiped it with the sleeves of his shirts. The nuns tried to get him to use a hankie, but he was a bush kid and he couldn't break the habit. They tied his arms behind his back. He sat in the classroom with snot running down his face. When he cried and made a goopy pool on the floor, they stood him up and strapped him and sat him back down after scraping at his nose with a coarse rag. As we bent our heads to our books we could hear him huffing, trying desperately to suck the snot back. But it was a medical condition and there was no relief. They began standing him at the front of the chapel, the classroom, the dining room with his hands wrapped behind him, making us witness the seeping track of the snot that bled down his face and neck into the collar of his shirt. He was six years old. He was from a people who had forged survival out of the bush as hunters, trappers, fishermen. That way of being was tied directly to the power they felt everywhere around them, and he'd been born to that, had learned it like walking. The nuns found him hanging from the rafters of the barn on a cold February morning. He'd wrapped his own hands behind his back with twists of rope before he'd jumped. They buried him in the graveyard that crept up to the edge of the bush. The Indian Yard. That's what the kids called it. Row on row of unmarked graves. Row on row of four- and five-foot indentations like a finger from Heaven had pressed them down. Dips in the earth. Holes they fell into.

Sheila Jack. They'd brought her all the way from Wikwemikong on Manitoulin Island. She was twelve. In the old way of her people, she'd been raised by her grandmother and been taught the traditional protocols of the medicine way. Her grandmother was a shaman, and Sheila would take her place one day. When she arrived at St. Germ's the kids were in awe of her. She walked into the school quietly, humbly, regally almost. It quieted us. We'd never seen anyone so composed, so assured, so peaceful. Something in her bearing reminded us about where we'd come from. We surrounded her like acolytes and that enraged the nuns. They thought Sheila was thumbing her nose at them and they set out to break her. They made her memorize the catechism and recite endlessly at the front of the classroom. If she made a mistake they struck her with a ruler, a strap or a hand and made her start over. She recited during meals, while she worked, while she walked. She wasn't allowed to speak to us. Her voice was consigned to the repetition of the texts. They woke her up from sound sleep and made her stand in the dormitory and say the words. When she began to mumble to herself we thought she was still at it. Then we began to notice that her words had no meaning. She'd walk the halls of St. Germ's muttering incomprehensible phrases and then burst out with a wild laugh, hitting herself with stinging slaps to the face before she returned to her vacant-faced mumbles. She lost the composed grace she'd arrived with. She got wild-eyed. Finally, she wandered away into the bush. The nuns found her three days later, knee deep in a bog, reciting, giggling, reciting again. That's what she was still doing when the car came and took her away to the crazy house.

Shane Big Canoe. They brought him to St. Germ's wrapped in ropes. When they untied him, he promptly ran away. I remember standing along the rail of the stairway with a dozen or so others when they brought him back. Two burly men from town had wrestled him into Father Quinney's office. We heard slaps, the whack of fists on flesh, the sound of wrestling and the crash of furniture. Then silence. When they walked him out past us, Shane's head was down and he didn't struggle. He plodded like an old man propped up by the elbows. They led him to the basement and locked him in the Iron Sister for ten days. It was called Contrition.

"I wouldn't want to be him," one of the kids whispered.

"No one comes back from there the same. Ever," said another.

"Perry Whiteduck said it's in the furthest darkest corner and the rats come at night and try to get you."

"He's gone. Right?" a girl asked.

"Yeah. He's in the Indian Yard."

"He didn't come back from his second trip there."

"He said it was so cold you breathe ice fog."

Shane Big Canoe was thirteen. His family was Metis from Saskatchewan and he was eight hundred miles from home. When he came out there was no more fight in his eyes. He held his raw-boned hands with their big knuckles in front of him, wringing them. He kept his head down, staring at his shoes. They'd find him at nights in the dormitory, huddled tight against the door where a sliver of light showed at its crack. It was the only place he could sleep. Close to that skiv of light, the glow of it on his face.

St. Germ's scraped away at us, leaving holes in our beings. I could never understand how the god they proclaimed was watching over us could turn his head away and ignore such cruelty and suffering.

13 ———

One afternoon, during some rare unsupervised time, a dozen of us escaped to the bottom of the ridge the school sat on. A small creek ran along the base of the ridge, curving up out of an inkpot lake and into a larger one. The creek was narrow, maybe three feet across, and shallow. It was a sucker creek. The fish swam up it to spawn in the bigger water and we went down there with burlap bags we'd taken from the barns. We could see the fish pushing up that water. It was thrilling. So much life, so much desperation, so much energy. We stood for a long time and just watched. Then some of us cut saplings and bent them around the inside lip of those sacks. We lowered the sacks into the water and pulled them up dripping and filled with fish. We watched the silvery, brown flash as they flopped out onto the bank, their puckered mouths flapping like wet kisses from fat aunties, their tails flipping and slapping against the ground. We pushed them back into the water and pulled up another sack. We did that four times. The fourth time we stood quietly, each of us lost in our thoughts, as the fish struggled for air, for life, for freedom. When we bent finally and took the fish in our hands to set them back into the water, most of us were crying. We turned as a group and began the long, sloping walk back up the ridge to the school. We walked with our hands cupped around our noses, breathing in the smell of those fish, pushing the slime of them around on our faces. We had no knives to clean them, flay them. We had no fire to smoke them over. We had no place to store them, no way to keep them. When they lay gasping on the grass, it was ourselves we saw fighting for air. We were Indian kids and all we had was the smell of those fish on our hands. We fell asleep that night with our noses pressed to our hands and as the days went by and the smell of those suckers faded, there wasn't a one of us that didn't cry for the loss of the life we'd known before. When the dozen of us cried in the chapel, the nuns smiled, believing it was the promise of their god that touched us. But we all walked out of there with our hands to our faces. Breathing in. Breathing in.

14 ———

I saw kids die of tuberculosis, influenza, pneumonia and broken hearts at St. Jerome's. I saw young boys and girls die standing on their own two feet. I saw runaways carried back, frozen solid as boards. I saw bodies hung from rafters on thin ropes. I saw wrists slashed and the cascade of blood on the bathroom floor and, one time, a young boy impaled on the tines of a pitchfork that he'd shoved through himself. I watched a girl calmly fill the pockets of her apron with rocks and walk away across the field. She went to the creek and sat on the bottom and drowned. That would never stop, never change, so long as that school stood in its place at the top of that ridge, as long as they continued to pull Indian kids from the bush and from the arms of their people. So I retreated. That's how I survived. Alone. When the tears threatened to erupt from me at night I vowed they would never hear me cry. I ached in solitude. What I let them see was a quiet, withdrawn boy, void of feeling.

───── 15

Father Gaston Leboutilier came to St. Jerome's the same year that I did. He was a young priest with a sense of humour that angered his fellow priests and the nuns, and a kindness and sense of adventure that drew the boys to him. He led hikes in the spring and summer. He took us camping for days at a time and when winter came he brought us hockey. He convinced Father Quinney to let him build a rink, outfit the older boys and start a team. Things changed at St. Jerome's after that, for one season of the year at least.

"Have you ever heard of hockey?" That was the first thing he said to me. I was sitting on the steps behind the kitchen as the other kids played in the fresh fallen snow.

"No. What is it?" I asked.

"It's a game," he said. "Maybe the greatest game. It's played on ice with skates and it's very fast, very exciting."

"Are there books about it?"

"A lot of books. I have some I could lend you. If you like what you read maybe you'll want to come and watch. We've built a rink and it's almost ready."

"I don't like games much."

He reached out and rubbed my hair. "So serious," he said. "We need to get you outside to watch. I guarantee you'll love it."

He smiled at me and I smiled back.

Father Leboutilier brought me hockey books and answered all my questions. His passion for the game was contagious. I read about heroes like Dit Clapper, Turk Broda, Black Cat Gagnon, "Sudden Death" Mel Hill and Ulcers McCool. Then there were more recent hockey gods, like Beliveau, Mahovlich and Rocket Richard. From the pages of those books I got the idea that hockey had an alchemy that could transform ordinary men into great ones. I will never forget the first time I watched the older boys play. The white glory of the rink. The sun was shining and the sky was pale blue. There wasn't a hint of wind. The air hung cold and crystalline as the boys pushed themselves around that oval to warm up, the huffing of their breath wreathing their heads. It reminded me of a locomotive, a steam-driven train bracing itself for release from the station.

The game started in a mad scramble. Reserve and bush boys made sudden crazy turns and spins as they chased the puck back and forth, and only the blast of Father Leboutilier's whistle returned things to a momentary calm. The players leaned forward on their sticks, eyes charcoal glints in the sunshine. The excitement in the air was so thick you could smell it. When the priest turned them loose to scrimmage, they broke with the abandon of mustangs. I never once looked at the puck. I kept my eyes glued to the boys, their sheer energy as they hurtled like comets. Father

Leboutilier skated loosely along the edges, pointing with his heavy hockey gloves or the blade of his stick. When he skated over to me, rubbing at his nose with the blunt thumb of a glove, his eyes were afire.

"There's an order to the game, Saul, though it might not be readily visible yet. There's a genuine rhythm under all this mayhem. When they grasp the rules you'll start to see it," he said.

"I see it already," I said.

"You do?"

"The lines," I said. "They create space. The space you have to move into to make it happen."

"You see that?"

"Yes."

And I did. I can't explain how it came to me, but I could see not just the physical properties of the game and the action but the intent. If a player could control a measure of space, he could control the game. The boys on the ice lurched and skimmed, oblivious to anything but the rubber sliding between their sticks. But I could see how a skater might move, where he might go to gain the advantage of space, how he might move the puck along to get it down ice and into the nest of twine that was the net.

There are stories of teachers among our people who could determine where a particular moose was, a bear, the exact time the fish would make their spawning runs. My great-grandfather Shabogeesick, the original Indian Horse, had that gift. The world spoke to him. It told him where to look. Shabogeesick's gift had been passed on to me. There's no other explanation for how I was able to see this foreign game so completely right away.

Father Leboutilier invited a small group of boys to his quarters, where he had a television. Few of us had seen one and we were thunderstruck. It was a box filled with apparitions, but once the game started we were too intent to pay attention to anything else. *Hockey Night in Canada* was the personification of magic. Ten men hurtling around a fenced perimeter with glorious speed. Cuts, switches, abrupt stops and misdirections. Hits, bumps, a focused grit and then the sweeping ballet of the open ice, the action funnelling down to a point where it became just the stick, the puck, the pads, the net, the red light and the klaxon sound of the buzzer that sent thousands erupting into glee. It thrilled me.

I begged to play after that. I begged to be taught to skate. But Father Quinney allowed only the older boys to play. I was eight and small. I asked again and again, and finally Father Leboutilier put his hand between my shoulder blades and leaned down to speak with me. His warm hand made me think of my grandmother's touch.

"There's nothing I can do, Saul," he said, quietly. "The rules are the rules. If I were to break them for you, it might prevent everyone from playing."

"But I want to learn it."

He smiled and pulled me forward into a hug. I closed my eyes and I almost cried for the memory of my father. He held me a long moment, then let me go.

"Can I look after the ice then?"

"You want to shovel snow?"

"Yes. Anything."

He looked out at the scramble of boys on the ice. "As long as you can keep up with your studies and your chores, I think I could arrange that."

16

Cleaning the rink became my assigned chore and I would rise to do it before anyone else in the school was up. Before the nuns, before the priests, before the cooks even got to the kitchen to start the oatmeal mush and dry toast that was our regular breakfast. I needed no alarm clock. I'd just wake and dress carefully in the dimness and creep downstairs in my stocking feet to the back door, where I kept my thin rubbers. I'd pull on a pair of extra wool socks Father Leboutilier had found for me and clamber into my winter coat and scarf and mitts and step out onto the back stairs. The edge of those mornings always caught at my lungs. The air was so cold and so pure it was hard to breathe. But I'd huff a breath or two and stamp my feet to get the blood moving and then walk slowly around the school and beyond the barn to where the rink stood. It was a purple world with only the varying degrees of light from the moon that allowed me to see. I'd get my shovel from where I'd stashed it in the snow, and I'd begin. I'd start at one side and push the snow to the foot of the boards that faced out to the field. Once the rink was scraped clear, I'd work my way along the length of the boards, pitching the snow piles over. I loved the feeling of my heaving breath and the clouds of fog that swirled around my head. I'd sweat. When I was done I would lean against the boards and examine my handiwork; the smooth grey plate of ice in the dim morning light. The idea of the game hanging in the frost. I was out on that rink every morning, even when the snow fell faster than I could shovel it.

At first I was simply grateful for my proximity to the game. But then I began to stash a hockey stick in the snow beside the boards. Once I'd made sure no one was around, I'd dig it out and run to the barn for a handful of the frozen horse turds I'd buried beside the door. I'd carry them back to the rink and drop them at one end. Then I'd take the stick and nudge one turd out of the heap and practice moving it back and forth, stickhandling, like I'd seen the players on *Hockey Night in Canada* do.

I moved it carefully so I wouldn't break the turd. I wanted to develop a soft touch, a deft weaving like the player Jean Beliveau, streaming up ice with the puck dangling on the blade of his stick like it was tied there on invisible twine. I made sure my stick made no sound against the ice, lest somebody discover me there. When the first turd eventually broke apart, I'd take another and I'd march up ice again with my substitute puck. I moved my feet as though I were skating, working the turd from side to side, making wider and wider sweeps. I got so I could slip it between my feet when I reached the end boards, spin around, cradle it in the middle of the blade and start back down the ice again. When all the turds were broken I'd flick the pieces over the boards with the wrist-shot motion I'd seen Dave Balon of the New York Rangers use. Then I'd stash my stick in the snow, shovel clear the evidence of my practice and head back to the building for breakfast and school.

At night in the dormitory, when all the other boys were asleep, I would get out of bed and stand in the aisle between the rows of cots, where the moonlight made the linoleum look like ice, and mimic the motion of stickhandling. I pictured myself barrelling across the blue line with the puck tucked neatly on the blade of my stick. I would throw a broad feint at the final defender and race in alone toward the goalie, who would begin to retreat slowly into the crease. I would shift my weight from foot to foot as I skated, dancing, wriggling, faking, the puck still nestled in the cradle of my blade. The space between the goalie and me would shrink and when I got about ten feet away I would draw the puck back behind my right leg. Then I would drive my weight forward onto my left leg and allow the momentum to bring the stick and puck forward. When the weight transfer was right, I'd snap my wrists and send the puck in a blur high into the right-hand corner, bulging the twine behind the helpless goaltender. Naturally, the force of my shot would take me to one knee. I would raise my arms in the hushed light of the dorm. My mouth would be open with glee and I would face the picture of Jesus hung there on the wall, my salvation coming instead through wood and rubber and ice and the dream of a game. I'd stand there, arms held high in triumph, and I would not feel lonely or afraid, deserted or abandoned, but connected to something far bigger than myself. Then I'd climb back into bed and sleep until the dawn woke me and I could walk back out to the rink again.

17 ———

Father Leboutilier was my ally. When the nuns and priests got too hard on me, he was there to mediate and defend me. By the second winter, when I was nine, I'd become braver. I took to stashing skates along with the stick. Father put me in charge of the equipment locker and it was my job now to keep things clean, to launder the sweaters, air out the gloves and pants and pads. I still rose before anyone else and made my way to the rink. There was always the ritual of shovelling the snow and clearing the ice, that solitary work of preparing to open the doors to a magical kingdom.

All of the skates were too big for me. So I stuffed the toes of a pair with newspaper to make them fit. Once they were laced tightly onto my feet I would grasp the edge of the boards and wobble along the length of the rink, then turn and wobble back the other way. Once I could travel the entire perimeter of the ice that way, I switched to a chair I took from the barn. I'd set it in front of me and lean on the back of it and push myself along. I always paid particular attention to the skating during *Hockey Night in Canada,* and I wanted to copy those motions. It was hard work, but I eventually got so I could push my way around the ice with that chair.

Then came the morning I let go of the chair.

I became a bird. An ungainly bird at first, but a creature of the air nonetheless. I leaned too far forward and had to save myself from falling, but I managed to propel myself along. In my mind I could see the way that I wanted my body to behave on skates and I worked toward that. For a week I practiced. Step and glide. Step. Glide. Step. Glide. I positioned my arms and concentrated on maintaining a stable posture. I'd picture the players I'd seen on TV, lock my gaze on the end boards and push myself toward them, gradually picking up speed.

I saw myself making the turn at the far end. Saw myself crossing my feet, one over the other, leaning to the inside, dropping the inside shoulder some, lifting my elbows higher and inscribing a perfect arc around the curve of the boards. Saw it as though I'd done it a hundred times. And then I did it. I cut around the net and followed the line of the boards and broke out of that long curve and lifted my hands straight up in the air as I glided into the open flare of the ice. Then I taught myself to go the other way.

I worked harder at clearing the ice to give myself more time to skate each day. I tore at that chore. I ran the width of the ice, pushing the snow into a pile along the boards. The labour made me wiry and tough. It gave my lungs a workout and cleared my mind of everything but the ice. As I laced on the skates my fingers actually trembled. Not from the cold but from the knowledge that freedom was imminent, that flight was at hand. I floated out onto a snow-white stage in a soliloquy of grace and motion. I loved it. Every time I skated I felt as though I had created the act. It was pure and new and startling.

The way I began was always the same. I would lean forward with my hands on my knees and stare at the ice, picking a spot on its surface. Then I would picture myself skating to that spot. I'd see myself making a wide circle that I'd bring in tighter and tighter before turning abruptly and skating out of the circle the other way. Then I would actually go and do it. My blades never made a sound. I couldn't let anyone discover what I was doing, so I learned how to skate soundlessly without the *chunk-chunk* of steel on ice the other boys made when they played the game. I learned to envision myself making moves before I tried them. If I could see myself doing it, then I could do it. It worked for any move. There was no explanation for how I could do what I did. I knew it as a mystery and I honoured it that way.

My grandmother had always referred to the universe as the Great Mystery.

"What does it mean?" I asked her once.

"It means all things."

"I don't understand."

She took my hand and sat me down on a rock at the water's edge. "We need mystery," she said. "Creator in her wisdom knew this. Mystery fills us with awe and wonder. They are the foundations of humility, and humility, grandson, is the foundation of all learning. So we do not seek to unravel this. We honour it by letting it be that way forever."

When I released myself to the mystery of the ice I became a different creature. I could slow down time, choose the tempo I needed whenever I launched myself into learning a new skill. I could hurtle down the ice at full speed and then bend time in upon itself to slow the turn, every muscle, every tendon, every sinew in my body remembering the movement, learning it, making it a part of me.

I learned to stop quickly on one skate. I learned to skate backwards, switching back and forth instantly, shifting my weight from foot to foot, making dazzling changes in direction. I set up horse turds in random patterns and learned to cut in around them from all sides. Every time, I would envision the move and then make it happen. I reached out with all the love in my heart and let it carry me deeper into the mystery.

Then I picked up the stick, using all of the skills I'd developed the winter before to stickhandle the horse turds around the ice. The turds were precious and I worked at not breaking them. I turned circles, first one way and then the other until I could make them faster and smaller. I practiced driving off one skate into high speed using as few strides as possible, balancing the turd on the blade of my stick. I shifted, I feinted, I faked. I raced across the ice with the silent swish of blades and cleared it of evidence as the turds broke with a short, sharp snap of my wrists.

I kept my discoveries to myself and I always made sure that I left the surface of the rink pristine. For the rest of the day, I'd walk through the dim hallways of the school warmed by my secret. I no longer felt the hopeless, chill air around me because I had Father Leboutilier, the ice, the mornings and the promise of a game that I would soon be old enough to play.

18 _____

Father Leboutilier worked the boys hard. He pushed them to do the drills and then to transfer that discipline into the scrimmage. He outlined what he wanted to see in the scrim of snow on the ice. Circles. Arrows. The math and the science of it all. Once they understood, they skated languidly back to their positions, their faces pulled into concentration. When the puck was dropped they moved deliberately, the scratchings and doodles on the ice suddenly coming to life. It was thrilling to see. They skated hard. They were big, lanky Indian boys and their angular faces were grave. As they pumped their legs and swung their arms in pursuit of the puck, zipping by me in a blur, they were warrior-like. When the whistle blew they turned as one. Some of them dropped onto the ice, legs splayed, chests heaving. Others leaned panting on the boards in front of me. Their faces burned with zeal and joy and their breathing was like the expelled air of mustangs. The clomp of their blades made me think of hoofs on frozen ground. This was the game. This gathering of brothers, of kin, joined by the exuberance of effort and challenge and strain, breathing the air that rose from the glacial face of a rink under a bleak sun.

The team was preparing for their first organized game against a town league team from White River. They practiced aggressively. Father Leboutilier whistled them down only when there was a flagrant misplay or a breach of the rules. The pace was breakneck. They poked and pulled and elbowed mightily to free the puck and send the game careering down the ice again. Then one afternoon someone screamed and a player fell to the ice clutching his leg. Father Leboutilier skated over quickly, knelt down and cradled the boy's head in his gloved hands. After a few minutes a couple of the boys helped the injured player to his feet. He leaned on them as they skated him slowly to the boards.

"I'm okay," he said.

"You can't stand on that ankle," Father Leboutilier said.

"I'm okay," the boy repeated.

"I'm sorry. I can't let you play when you're hurt."

"We ain't got no one else. How you gonna make a team?" the boy asked.

The words were out of me before I'd thought them through. "I'll go in for Wapoose," I said.

The Father looked at me in surprise. "You skate, Saul?"

"Yes."

"How did you learn?"

"By myself. In the mornings. After I cleared the ice."

The others were watching me, their eyes glittering obsidian from beneath the rims of their helmets. I was just the ice cleaner, the Zhaunagush in their midst. They'd been content enough to just leave me alone but I was still the outsider. The Father rubbed at his chin with his glove and stared out across the field. "Well, I suppose you can fill in for the scrimmage."

I ran to the snowbank to retrieve my stick. When Father Leboutilier handed me Wapoose's skates, I went to the barn to get the wadding of paper I kept there and stuffed it in their toes then slipped my feet in and laced them up tight. The Father was grinning as I leaped over the boards. I skated once around the ice. Slowly. Getting my legs under me. Father Leboutilier nodded, and when I got back to where the team was, he put a hand on my shoulder and directed me to Wapoose's place on the right wing.

I could barely breathe. My whole body was quivering. Once the puck was dropped I lagged behind the play to study it. When the players moved up ice I skated on my wing. The other boys ignored me.

I stayed at the edge of the scrimmage, the play rolling its pattern out in front of me. Then, suddenly, I saw it clearly. I saw the direction of the game before it happened and I moved to that spot. Now I bent to my skating, spreading my feet a little wider and keeping the full length of my stick blade on the ice.

There was a collision at the blue line and the puck squirted free. It spun like a small planet in a universe of white. Everyone reacted at the same time. I could hear the clomp of their blades. But I pushed hard, evenly, and I was at full speed in three strides. I scooped the puck onto my stick and cradled it as I pumped with my other arm. The goalie yelped and backed slowly toward the mouth of the net. I whisked across the blue line and there was only me, the puck and the net. I was flying, skating as fast as I could go, and then time slowed to a crawl. I could hear my breath, the yells of the other boys behind me, feel the pump of blood in my chest, see the eyes of the goalie squinting in concentration.

When I was twelve feet out I leaned back on the heels of my skates and pushed the puck out in the space between my knees. I shuffled it back and forth like Beliveau. I wriggled my shoulders and then I pulled a broad feint to my left and the goalie took it, sliding over on one padded knee with the paddle of his stick on the ice. Once he'd committed I tucked the puck back neatly between my legs, like I'd done so many mornings with the horse turds, reached back with my stick and caught the puck in the middle of my blade. I flicked my wrist and the puck slipped neatly into the right angle where the crossbar met the post.

I spun on my skates and slid backwards into the boards behind the net. I was too shocked to raise my arms.

The other players turned in a long slow curve to stare at me in amazement. Father Leboutilier stood at centre ice, a giant grin on his face.

"You taught yourself the game, Saul?"

"Yes. From books and the games on television."

"That was a pretty snazzy move. You taught yourself that?"

"Yes. I practiced stickhandling with turds."

He laughed. He rubbed my head with one glove and then motioned the other boys over. "Can you play centre, Saul?" Father Leboutilier asked.

"Like Beliveau?"

He grinned. "Yes. Like Beliveau."

"I can try."

"Good. Ottertail, you take the right wing."

"I play centre," Ottertail said with a hard look at me.

"Let Saul try it. Just for the scrimmage."

Father Leboutilier blew his whistle and I lined up to take the first faceoff of my life. I lost the draw, but once the scrimmage began, that curious sense of being able to anticipate the play took over. The puck seemed to follow me. Father Leboutilier just let us skate and after a while our plays became sharp and crisp and we were all together in the thrill of the game. When Father Leboutilier finally whistled us to a stop, the older boys skated to the boards and leaned there. I dawdled behind them, unsure of what to do. But as I drew near they made a spot for me among them. We stood there like stallions home from the range.

———— 19

Father Quinney and Sister Ignacia protested at first about my age and small size and the effect that breaching rules would have on the rest of the children. But once Father Quinney saw me play, things changed.

"He has a God-given gift for it, Sister," he said when Sister Ignacia pressed the issue.

I kept my morning job, but now I wore the skates when I shovelled. Once the ice was cleared I would pull one of the nets from its place on the snowbank and dangle my boots from the corners and practice hitting them with wrist shots. I created skating drills for myself. I did figure eights in both directions. I did them skating backwards. I set up lines of pucks and practiced cutting between them at as fast a speed as I could manage, switching between skating forward and backwards as I did it. I'd watched figure skaters on Father Leboutilier's television, and I started to mimic their movements in my play. I made spinning turns, abrupt changes of direction on one foot. There wasn't a nuance that I didn't try to incorporate into what felt like flying, being borne across the sky on great wings. I loved that. I was a small boy with outsized skates, and in the world that hockey had created I found a new home.

I'd never heard from my parents. Maybe they couldn't find me. Maybe their shame over abandoning us in the bush was too great. Or maybe the drink had taken them over as easily as hockey had claimed me. Some nights I felt crippled by the ache of loss. But I knew that loneliness would be dispelled by the sheen of the rink in the sunlight, the feel of cold air on my face, the sound of a wooden stick shuffling frozen rubber.

———— 20

We played the town team three weeks after Father Leboutilier first let me skate with the bigger boys. My teammates laughed when they saw me in my uniform. Another town team had donated their old sweaters, and I looked as though I were drowning in mine. It hung as though there were no bones to me. My outsized skates and full-sized stick made me looked even odder. Father Leboutilier had tried to convince me to cut my stick down some, but the longer shaft felt more familiar to me.

The game was held in the White River arena. We'd only ever played outdoors and the heat in the dressing rooms made the air feel heavy in our lungs. We were used to suiting up in the full chill. We were used to allowing the cold to prepare us, and those first circles on the ice, the rush of blood to our muscles, the gradual warming from the effort, were how we readied ourselves. In the arena, yellow lights were above us instead of the sun, and rafters instead of clouds. There was glass above the boards and behind the nets instead of chicken wire.

When I skated out at the tail end of our team I could see people in the stands pointing at me and laughing.

"The Indian school brought their mascot!"

"Is he a squirt? Nah. He's a dribble!"

Father Leboutilier huddled us all together on the bench and I listened intently to screen out the taunts.

"These boys are a skilled team," the Father said. "They've been playing organized games since they were six. This is your first organized game. So play it for fun. Play it to learn. Play it as a team and you can't lose."

There were twelve of us. Two sets of five and a pair of goalies. We were nervous. I could see that in my teammates' faces. As soon as the puck was dropped it was obvious how outmatched we were. The town team moved the puck quickly. Their passes were crisp and on target. They scored within the first minute. But before long, sitting there on the bench, I felt that curious sense of vision descend on me. I could see. I could see what they were going to do before they did it. By the time Father Leboutilier called for my line, I was ready.

The crowd howled when they saw me skate to the centre line to take the faceoff. Their centreman scowled and slapped my stick with his own.

"Shrimp," he said. "Stay out of my way."

He won the draw and the puck skittered back to their defensemen. I skated easily with the play as it made its way down ice. We gained control of the puck and started our own rush, but that broke down at their blue line. I watched the other team closely, and when the puck went into the right-hand corner of our end after a blocked shot, I knew I had them. I pushed off hard, breaking into the clear on a hard angle in front of our defenseman. I yelled. He saw me and flipped the puck toward me. I snared it easily with one hand and turned up ice at the same time.

Three of their players were ahead of me. When the left-winger tried to check me, I went left. I poked the puck back to the right, between his legs, and stepped around him. Their defense was backing up and a dozen feet separated us. I outskated the first boy. He came with me as I flashed across the ice, but I cut hard at the boards on both blades at a sharp angle, the puck on my backhand, and left him there. The second boy skated backwards as I straightened and aimed right for him. I stared at his chest and let the puck dangle at the end of my blade. I could feel his eyes go there, and when he lunged I spun, tucked the puck between my legs, picked it up as I came out of the spin and was clear. I could hear the crowd yelling at their team to stop me. I covered the sixty feet to the net in no time. Their goalie had backed up into the crease. I leaned to the right. He followed me. In my mind I saw my school boot dangling by its laces from the top right corner of the net. I leaned hard on my right skate and snapped off a wrist shot at the same time. The goalie flung up his glove hand but it was too late. The puck skimmed into the top corner of the net.

The arena went crazy. The klaxon buzzer sounded, the red light flashed, their players slammed their sticks on the ice, the crowd roared. I was lost in a wild celebration of arms and sticks and helmets. Father Leboutilier was standing at the open gate to our bench as I skated over, his face was red with excitement. He stopped me and put his hands on my shoulder pads.

"That was beautiful," he said. "You were beautiful."

I sat on the bench and basked in that. When I leaped back onto the ice, it was with determination to earn the Father's praise again. There was no laughter from the crowd when I took the puck this time. Instead, they yelled at their team to stop me, to hit me, to crush me. But when the players tried I simply skated faster. No one could touch me. I scored twice more and made the passes that earned us another two goals and we won that game by a single goal. I was applauded as I left the ice, and in the dressing room my teammates gaped. I just offered a small grin, then bent to my skates and began to unlace them.

Father Leboutilier came and sat down beside me and leaned back against the wall with his legs thrown straight out in front of him. He put a hand on my back and patted me.

"Saul," he said quietly, "the game loves you."

I sat with the Father's hand on my back, listening to the excited chatter of the team as they recreated the game. The game loves you, he'd said, and right there, right then, I loved it back.

———— 21

St. Jerome's was hell on earth. We were marched everywhere. In the mornings, after the priests had walked
through the dorms ringing cowbells to scare us awake, we
were marched to the latrines. We stood in lines waiting
our turn at the toilets—a dozen of them for a hundred and
twenty boys. Some of us soiled our pants during the wait,
because we were strapped if we left our beds at night. We
had half an hour to wash, make our beds and prepare ourselves for the march to chapel. There we sat dully in our
seats while Father Quinney said a mass in Latin. At the end
he pronounced the greatness of the Catholic god.

"We brought you here to save you from your heathen
ways, to bring you to the light of the salvation of the one
true God. What you learn here will raise you up, make you
worthy, cleanse your body and purify your spirit."

When he was satisfied that the message had been
pounded into us, we were marched to the dining room for
breakfast. The boys and the girls sat on opposite sides of
the room. We stood behind our chairs until everyone had
their bowl of lumpy, tasteless porridge, slice of dry toast
and watery glass of powdered milk. Then one of the priests
would say grace, and we would sit and eat in silence. Not

one of us could resist risking a beating by sneaking a peek at the nuns and priests at their table, eating their eggs, bacon or sausage. The smell of it would waft over us while we choked down our gruel then sat with our hands at our sides until they were finished eating and we were marched to our work details.

They called it a school, but it was never that. Most of our days were spent in labour. Even the youngest of us had to work. The girls were kept busy in the kitchen, where they baked bread to be sold in town, or in the sewing rooms, where they made our clothing out of the heavy, scratchy material the school got from the army. The boys mucked out the stalls of the cows and horses, hoed the fields, harvested the vegetables or worked in the carpentry shop, where they built the furniture the priests sold to the people of White River. We spent an hour in the classroom each day to learn the rudimentary arithmetic and English that would enable us to secure manual labour when we "graduated" from the school. There were no grades or examinations. The only test was our ability to endure. Since I could already read and speak English when Father Leboutilier came along, I was given access to books from the town library. But the others had to read from primers and never gained facility with the language. Kids were routinely strapped for giving the wrong answer. In front of the entire class, kids were turned to face the wall, made to pull their pants down to their ankles, bent over with their hands on their knees and whipped raw. Boys and girls alike, except that the girls were allowed to keep their underthings on.

"I seen more little brown nuts than a squirrel," Lenny Mink said to me once. "And more dark cracks than the river at spring breakup." He was funny, that Lenny Mink. He died when they were trying to clear a stump from the end of a field and a tractor chain snapped. Lenny's head was split wide open in front of all those boys. There wasn't a funeral. There never was for kids who died. His body just disappeared and none of the priests or nuns said anything about him again.

We were like stock. That's how we were treated. Fed, watered, made to bear our daily burden and secured at night. Anybody who shirked or complained was beaten in front of everyone. That was perhaps the biggest crime: making us complicit through our mute and helpless witness. Sometimes older boys or girls would jump in and try to stop a beating, but they would be pummelled and bloodied and led away, never to be seen again.

We lived under constant threat. If it wasn't the direct physical threat of beatings, the Iron Sister or vanishing, it was the dire threat of purgatory, hell and the everlasting agony their religion promised for the unclean, the heathen, the unsaved. Those of us who remembered the stories told around our people's fires trembled in fear at the images of hell, damnation, fire and brimstone.

I was never sent to the Iron Sister, but I saw it once. Father Leboutilier and I were stashing the hockey gear in the school's basement. I had an armload of equipment as I walked behind him down the stairs. We turned a corner, and there it was. It was shaped like a shoebox, long and flat with a small grille in the door. I could see that it wasn't high enough to allow even the smallest child to stand, or even kneel. I walked toward it, and the iron was cold to my touch.

"Come away from there, Saul," the Father said from behind me.

"Why do they have this?" I asked

"They lack charity."

When your innocence is stripped from you, when your people are denigrated, when the family you came from is denounced and your tribal ways and rituals are pronounced backward, primitive, savage, you come to see yourself as less than human. That is hell on earth, that sense of unworthiness. That's what they inflicted on us.

The beatings hurt. The threats belittled us. The incessant labour wearied us, made us old before our time. The death, disease and disappearances filled us with fear. But perhaps what terrified us most were the nighttime invasions.

They would start with the swish of slippered feet along the floorboards or the hems of cassocks and gowns as the predators hurried through the dorms. We'd push our faces into our pillows or bury our heads beneath our blankets to drown out the surf of woe that came each night. First, there would be the creak of bed springs as the adults sat. Soft whispers, cajoling, and then the rustling sounds that tattooed themselves onto our brains, the cries of distress, the sound of skin sliding against skin and the low adult growls were born of a hunger none of us could ever understand. Sometimes three or four boys would be visited like that. Sometimes only one. Other times boys would be led from the dorms. Where they went and what happened to them was never spoken of. In the daylight we would look at each other blankly, so that we would not cause any further shame. It was the same for the girls.

"God's love," Angelique Lynx Leg whispered one day.

We were shelling peas on opposite sides of a five-gallon pail. She said it so quietly I looked up to see if she was addressing me. She wasn't. In her hands, a slick green shell she rubbed with the nub of a thumb. "God's love," she said again, and then looked at me with eyes as deep and empty as the eyes of a doll. "What Sister brings at night. What Father brings. To bless me. To nourish me."

I watched as a single tear flowed out of the corner of her eye, burst fully formed against her brown skin. She reached up with one finger. Then she held that finger up in front of her face and looked at it, tasted it with her tongue and then bent to the task of shelling peas again. She was nine years old and all I felt was hollow.

22 ———

When I hit the ice I left all of that behind me. I stepped onto the ice and Saul Indian Horse, the abandoned Ojibway kid, clutched in the frozen arms of his dead grandmother, ceased to exist.

Father Leboutilier loved the game more than anybody. When he coached us or watched the televised games, he lost the solemn priestly facade and became a boy again, licking his lips in anticipation. His relish was infectious.

So it didn't surprise me when he began to show up at my early morning solo practices. He'd wait until I had scraped the ice clear and done my warm-ups, then lace up his own skates and join me. During those sessions I learned how to transfer what I could see in my head into my feet and my hands. Father Leboutilier taught me how to take a pass on my backhand without looking then switch it to my forehand to take a shot. He taught me how to snap off wrist shots like rockets with fast passes he fed me from behind the net. I learned how to fire accurately off either foot while still in motion and he showed me how my skates could help me handle the puck on the attack. As I demonstrated each new technique, each step up in understanding, the delight on his face was my reward.

"Hockey is like the universe, Saul," he said one day. "When you stand in the dark and look up at it, you see the placid fire of stars. But if we were right in the heart of it, we'd see chaos. Comets churning by. Meteorites. Star explosions. Things being born, things dying. Chaos, Saul. But that chaos is organized. It's harnessed. It's controlled. What you can't see under all the action, the speed, the mayhem, is the great spirit of this game. That's what makes you so extraordinary. You have that spirit within you."

I took his words to heart and I practiced diligently.

Our school team played the town team a few more times that winter, and we won handily. Word had gotten around how well we played, and even Father Quinney attended a few games. My vision grew even sharper the more I played. There would always come a moment when the game would swing to me and I would find the puck on my stick. I came to expect that, relied on it.

Winter ended and the rink melted back into the furrows of the field. But I kept getting up early. I began to run. I'd run down the curving gravel road to the bottom of the ridge and then up its harsh slope. When I got to the top I would turn and face the school while I caught my breath, and then I would turn and head through the bush to the lowland, where there was a beaver lodge. I'd watch the vee of swimming beavers, listen to ducks and mergansers, and think about what Father Leboutilier had said about my underlying spirit.

When I told him what I was doing, he joined me. We ran every morning. He told me how important it was for a player to have strong thighs. He'd been to the Montreal

Forum and met the astonishingly fast junior star Yvan Cournoyer in the Junior Canadiens' dressing room.

"His thighs were like loaves of bread. Huge. He even had to have his pants tailored for him. He is the fastest player I have ever seen, Saul."

We started to do wind sprints up the face of the ridge. Once I could do a dozen in a row, he took me along the ridge to where boulders were thrown in a mad jumble at its base. I ran that talus every day. Leaping and bounding between the rocks was exhilarating, and we made a game of it. I tapped into the spirit of hockey in those tough training runs.

One day when I was working in the barn, I discovered a sheet of linoleum stuffed in the back of the loft. As I wiped the chaff away, it felt like ice on my palm. I carried it out to the area where the hockey nets were stored and placed it about twenty feet in front of one of them. Then I took a stick and a puck and began snapping wrist shots at the net. Father Leboutilier ran interference for me with Sister Ignacia and got me free time to practice in the hour before the evening meal. It was a joy to find the game in the heat of summer, and when I saw a workman cutting off sections of three-inch pipe with a welding torch one afternoon, I asked if he could cut me a couple. Those rings weighed far more than a regular puck and I stickhandled with them and worked on my wrist shot until my wrists and forearms were rock hard. When I showed Father Leboutilier, he laughed.

"Marvellous," he said and roughed my hair.

The Father got some boys in the wood shop to cut six holes in a sheet of plywood, one at each corner, right and left, top and bottom, one square in the middle at the bottom, and one in the centre top. I practiced shooting the heavy rounds of pipe at each of those holes. I worked hard at that. I practiced until I could feather the steel through each of those gaps. Then Father Leboutilier started calling out the holes to me.

"Top right!"

I'd sail a ring of pipe through that hole. He'd roll it back, then call out another hole. My shots grew pinpoint accurate and fast off the stick. When we switched back to regular pucks, the rubber was a blur.

The other boys got wind of what I was doing and showed up to watch. Eventually they joined in and we held tournaments. Each hole had a point value and we each took twenty shots. The one with the highest points won. I went through the end of that summer and the fall undefeated. And in the gathering gloom of those evenings we all grew closer. I ceased to be the Zhaunagush. I became Saul Indian Horse, Ojibway kid and hockey player. I became a brother. I basked in the glow of this regard. In our laughter, teasing and rough camaraderie, I found another expression of the spirit of the game. We'd head back to the main building for the evening meal, jockeying, nudging, poking each other. Wrapped in the aura of freedom that the game offered us, we'd grin at each other over the hash and skimpy stews. Brothers. Joined by the promise of steel blades forming swirls in snow and ice.

23 ———

We were all a year older by the time winter came. I was almost thirteen. Our team looked bigger and more powerful when we took to the ice. Father Leboutilier had canvassed the other towns in the region and amassed a ragtag assortment of cast-off gear. Not all of our jerseys matched and they were stained and torn and ragged.

"Hey Father," someone yelled from the seats at our first town game. "Good joke. Holey sweaters!"

There was laughter all around. But it stopped with our first shift. The summer of workouts had made all of us stronger and faster—the other boys had often joined Father Leboutilier and me for our training runs. Shooting the iron pucks off the linoleum had strengthened our shots and passes. When the boys asked me how I was able to do certain things, like stopping on one skate, or switching quickly from forward to backwards skating, they listened closely when I explained it, and then practiced it diligently too. We were in far better condition than the town kids. We brought a supple strength to our game now.

The speed I had from the year before had increased twelve-fold. That first game, one of the town players poked the puck away from our defense and rumbled up ice all alone. I was caught behind their goal. But I caught him by the time he reached our blue line. I cut in front of him in a wide circle with my stick flat on the ice. I swept the puck off his stick and began skating back the other way. Everyone, including my own teammates was stunned. I skated by them in a blur and sped in alone on the goaltender. I snapped a wrist shot off from the bottom of the faceoff circle and beat him low on his stick side.

We won that game and the next three. After that some men from town showed up at the school and asked permission for me to play on their midget town team. I was stunned. So was Father Leboutilier.

"Midget players are sixteen and seventeen," he told them.

"That boy is too fast for the bantams and he's way too good for the peewees," one of the men said. "Our midget team is competitive and we could use him."

"He's only thirteen," the Father said.

"He plays older and bigger."

"His first organized game was last winter."

"You'd never know it."

It took a hefty donation to the school to get Father Quinney to agree to let me play. Father Leboutilier drove me to practices and games in the old station wagon the nuns used for errands.

"It feels different," I said one day.

"What does, Saul?" the Father asked.

"The game."

"How?"

"I don't know. I feel kinda scared playing in town all the time. Like they expect me to be something that I don't know how to be."

"They expect you to be a good hockey player."

"Yeah. But there it feels like they want more than that."

"Like what, Saul?"

"I don't know. I guess that's what scares me."

The town team was coached by Levi Deiter, who ran the hardware store. But Father Leboutilier and I still went over things every morning on the school rink. He taught me a couple dozen different ways to ice the puck, to send it out of my team's zone and down the length of the rink when the pressure was too intense. I learned how to make passes to myself using the boards, to rag the puck effectively if our team was short-handed. He showed me how to work the puck along the boards when a mash of players converged and how to use my body for leverage even though I was smaller than the players I faced. And he showed me how to take a hit and keep skating.

"Two essential things," he said. "Always keep your stick on the ice and always keep your legs moving."

The Father and I discovered ways for me to catch my breath, conserve my energy and rest, all while staying in motion and keeping myself in the play. I found I could go for longer and longer shifts. I scored a few goals in my first few games with the White River Falcons, but it was my passes that got people's attention. I'd chosen thirteen as my number because no one else wanted it. The people in the bleachers never learned my name, but I could overhear their comments from the bench.

"That thirteen's got eyes in the back of his head."

"How did thirteen know Stevie was open on the right side?"

"Thirteen's good for an Indian."

indian horse

I played ten games in total for White River. We won seven of them. I put up fourteen points in those ten games, most of them assists on passes no one saw coming. The five goals I scored were all on wrist shots. The other players relied on big booming slap shots like they'd seen Bobby Hull do on TV. I admired Hull's thunder too, but I preferred the hair-trigger release of a good wrist shot.

I gave myself to the game utterly. I loved the talks with Father Leboutilier in that old station wagon, the smell of musty gear and spit and sweat, the muttered curses and high-voiced shouts from the bench. I thrived on the sound of sticks banging applause against the boards, skate blades pounding a tattoo on the floor of the bench when a move electrified the team, and the feel of thick, padded gloves tousling my hair. In the spirit of hockey I believed I had found community, a shelter and a haven from everything bleak and ugly in the world.

But the world of hockey in the early 1960s was a closed one, as it turned out. When Father Leboutilier arrived for the eleventh game, Levi Deiter was waiting for us alone in the lobby of the rink. He had his hands stuffed in his pockets and he wouldn't look me in the eye. He motioned to Father Leboutilier, and they retreated to a corner by the trophy case. I stood there with my gear bag in my hand, wondering what the big secret was. They talked for a long time and I could see that the Father was growing agitated. Finally, he laid a hand on Levi Deiter's shoulder. When Deiter looked up I could see tears in his eyes and I looked down at my feet in embarrassment. Father Leboutilier walked slowly back toward me, his lips pinched together.

"Did the game get cancelled?" I asked.

"There is no game, Saul," the Father said softly. Just then my right-winger walked by with his gear bag in his hand.

"But Jimmy's here."

"I know, but there is no game for you. They don't want you to play anymore, Saul."

"What? I'm the best they got."

"I know. That's why they don't want you to play."

"I don't understand."

"The parents of other players want their own kids to play."

"They do play."

"Yes. But they're not on the ice as much as you are."

I stared out at the glare of the ice beyond the glass of the lobby and at the banks of empty seats. Other players sauntered through the doors, but when they saw me they lowered their gaze and walked faster. Father Leboutilier and I stood there amidst the whirr of the heater, the shouts and teasing of the players in the dressing room, the crunch of snow as cars pulled up outside. Finally, he put a hand on my shoulder and guided me out the door. I stood in the cold outside the station wagon while he slung my gear bag in the back. I could only stare at the arena. We didn't talk on the drive to the school until we were almost there. I looked out at the rolling fields of white interspersed with copses of trees and thickets of bush.

"It's because I'm Indian, isn't it?"

He drove with both hands on the wheel, looking straight ahead. "Yes," he said.

"Do they hate me?"

"They don't hate you, Saul."

"Well, what, then?"

"They think it's their game."

"Is it?"

I could hear the crack of our tires in the frost on the road. "It's God's game," he said.

"Where's God now, then?" I asked.

He gripped the wheel harder as the ruddy face of St. Jerome's slid into view at the crest of the ridge.

24 ———

I spent the rest of that winter skating with the boys from the school. Our games were fast but scrambled. I'd send the puck out to a lagging winger and it would sit there spinning uselessly. Or I'd burst in on goal and I'd see the goaltender give up as soon as I crossed the blue line. Father Leboutilier and I still watched televised games in his quarters, and he continued to point things out to me. Whenever I had the ice to myself I'd practice those things over and over. The Father joined me sometimes. He was the only one who could really challenge me. As winter began to dwindle into spring, I felt defeated.

But one day as the team scrimmaged, I looked up to see a man standing at the boards with Father Leboutilier. He was watching me closely. He was Ojibway. I could tell that from the cut of his features and his thick upper body. I was treating that scrimmage as though it were the last game I would ever play, because I didn't know what the next winter would bring. So I skated with all of the joy I had in me. I whirled and sped away with the puck. I yelled in jubilation. Near the end I just flew around the perimeter as fast as I could go. When Father Leboutilier whistled us to a stop he motioned me over to the boards.

"Nice game," the man standing with him said. "Fred Kelly."

He took off his mitt and we shook hands.

"Mr. Kelly has a tournament team, Saul. In Manitou-wadge," Father Leboutilier said.

"The Moose," Fred said.

"What's a tournament team?" I asked.

Fred Kelly leaned toward me. He squinted into the glare of the sun on the ice and pointed at the end boards. The chicken wire had begun to sag from errant slap shots striking it all winter. "We play Native tournaments. Every reserve across our territory has a team, and we play on outside rinks just like this one. Every weekend in the winter, right up to breakup, or to when our forwards start having to wear flippers instead of skates."

He laughed; a big manly sound that just erupted from him. "Anyway, we love hockey. Trouble is, the mill town teams don't want anything to do with us. They won't play us even though we're good enough. Our kids don't get to play in their town leagues either."

"Because they think it's their game," I said.

Kelly spat tobacco juice at the ice. He squinted at Father Leboutilier and grimaced. "Yeah," he said. "That's pretty much it."

"I know about that."

"Father told me. What I seen here, it's no wonder they're scared to play you."

I waited for him to continue. There didn't seem to be anything for me to say.

"When they're old enough, and if they're good enough, our kids can play with the travelling team. The Moose.

Most of them are seventeen, eighteen, and they play junior-level hockey. Fast, hard hockey," he said. "The reserves take a lot of pride in their teams. They take pride in being good hosts, too, so there's always a warm bed and good food. We bunk with families. Even if it's fifty below, a crowd turns out to watch. It's tough to play in the wind and snow, but if you love the game like our guys do, you'll play through anything. Right now, we're down a centre on the third line. Wondered if maybe you'd wanna come and play with us?"

I was thunderstruck. All I could manage was to let my mouth hang open.

"Saul, Fred lived here at the school for eight years. So did his wife, Martha," Father Leboutilier said. "I wrote him after the town barred you from playing. Fred wants you to go and live with his family and play hockey for the Moose, to play with a real team where the game can challenge you. Would you like that?"

I felt as though the world had slipped out of orbit. I could find no words.

"The Kellys would be your legal guardians, Saul. That means you could leave here and go to Manitouwadge, attend a regular school. You'd have a home, Saul. A real home."

"I could play hockey?" It was all I could squeeze out.

"All you can handle," Fred said.

"What if I'm not good enough?"

Fred laughed again and slapped me lightly on the back. "I don't think that's anything you ever have to worry about."

SISTER IGNACIA was vehement in her disgust with the idea.

"Surrendering him to the influence of a soulless game is not what we were directed to do here," she said.

"But the game offers him a chance at a better life. He has an amazing natural talent. It could take him far," Father Leboutilier said.

"The game is savage. We were sent to cleave the savage from them."

"I thought we were sent to offer counsel, and the means to a better life?"

"You are naive."

"Perhaps. But he will have the benefit of a good home and good schooling. We will have achieved our mission."

It was Father Quinney, in the end, who made the whole thing possible. He'd stayed silent while Sister Ignacia and Father Leboutilier sawed back and forth. Then he got up and walked to the window, standing there with his hands clasped behind his back. When he turned to face us he looked pensive.

"Our Lord works His magic in particular ways. Strange to some. Downright odd at times." He returned to his chair to scan the guardianship papers.

"I don't know why He chose to grace this boy with the skills he has. But I have witnessed his ability myself. That pass he made on the backhand through three sets of legs and sticks to that open winger in the last White River game? That was a minor miracle."

He grinned at the recollection. Sister Ignacia scowled. Father Quinney set the papers down in front of him. "The boy has no family that we know of. He has shown himself to be a disciplined student, a devoted reader. To hold him back from nurturing a gift that is divine in nature would be counterproductive to what we set out to achieve. Do you want to go, Saul? Will you pay heed to what the Kellys ask of you? Will you honour their direction as you would honour ours?"

I looked around at all those adult faces, lingering on Father Leboutilier's. I'd never been offered choice before. "All right," I said. "I'll go."

I WALKED OUT of that room and back to the dormitory one last time to collect the few things I could call possessions. Already I could feel St. Jerome's losing its hold on me. I was almost fourteen. I was being freed. But I was scared too, and I moved through those dim hallways with something akin to regret. This was the only place I'd known for the past five years. And I'd be leaving Father Leboutilier behind.

Most of the kids were working at that hour. No one was about except for one girl I did not know, wiping down the walls with a sponge. She was nine, maybe ten, but the smock sagging to her knees and her dark stockings and shapeless shoes made her look like an old woman. I coughed, and she looked for a moment. There was no recognition on her face, no expression except surrender. When I made a small wave she raised her chin an inch or so, gazed at me with dark, empty eyes and then reached down to squeeze her sponge again.

I carried my little canvas bag of belongings down the stairs and out to the foyer, where Fred Kelly and Father Leboutilier waited. "I'm ready," I said. When we reached

Fred Kelly's car, the Father looked off toward the trees at the end of the field. I saw him swallow hard before he turned to me. I didn't know what else to do so I stuck my hand out. Father Leboutilier gave it a firm shake, then pulled me to him. I felt his hand cradle the back of my head.

"Go with God," he whispered.

25 ———

Manitouwadge means "Cave of the Great Spirit" in Ojibway. That was funny, because it was mining that gave the town its life. Everyone in Manitouwadge worked in the mines or the sawmills, and Fred Kelly had brought his family there from the Pic River reservation to join the thirty other Ojibway families who lived in a neighbourhood on the outskirts called Indian Town by the locals. Its residents called it the Rez. I'd learn fast enough that an invisible line was drawn across the intersection of Sanderson Road and Township Road Eleven that everyone regarded as part of the local geography. The town proper was populated by tough, narrow-minded men and their loyal women and their callow kids, all rough-and-tumble and rude. It was a place of Saturday night fights in the parking lot outside Merle's Old Time Saloon, wild country dances at the Legion Hall, bass boats, snowmobiles, motorcycles and random games of Broom-a-Buck, the redneck game of leaning out the window of a car or truck to swat Indians on the sidewalk or the road. Fifty points for a head shot. Twenty for any other part of the body. I'd learn all of this later. That first day, in the late winter of 1966, all I saw was a town drenched in the seeping grey of spring breakup.

The outdoor rink behind Fred Kelly's house was almost gone, but he showed it to me first thing. His back yard was huge, ending at an outcropping of pink granite, and the rink was full-sized. Seeing it eased the ache in my chest a little.

A tall, spare woman wearing a big smile opened the back door and stood with her arms wrapped around herself, shifting from foot to foot in the icy breeze. "Fred, for Pete's sake. The boy needs food before he needs hockey. Bring him in and let's meet him proper."

Fred laughed and pushed me lightly in the direction of the house. "Ma's first rule is food. She cooks up a storm too."

The house was full of people. The Kellys had three sons. Garrett and Howard were married, and they were there with their wives and children. The youngest, Virgil, was a hulking seventeen year old. When Fred introduced me, Virgil squinted in a friendly way and looked me up and down.

"Kinda small," he said as he shook my hand.

"He plays bigger," Fred said.

"He'll wanna."

Virgil was the captain of the Moose. "It's kinda like being a chief," he said. "It's all about family and who you know. Garrett was captain before me. Kind of went down the line. The guys? They're not gonna take to you right away."

"Why?" I asked.

"Couple reasons," he said. By now we were sitting at the kitchen table with our soup and bannock, real food that I ate hungrily. "First is you're not from here and you're taking a spot away from someone else. Second is you're a sawed-off little runt and they're gonna think they have to protect you, stand up for you."

"They won't." I said.

"You'll have to prove that. My dad says you got a hell of a game, but they'll make you prove that too. It won't be easy."

We ate in silence after that. When we were finished, Martha showed me to my room, and we went shopping for clothing. I'd never had anyone spend money on me, and it felt odd standing in front of mirrors with the cardboard feel of new pants against my legs, and crisp new shirts around my throat. Fred took me to the sporting goods store next and bought me my first gear. Now I had skates that fit properly. I had a stick right for my size and equipment that didn't drape over me. I couldn't wait to hit the ice and see how it felt to be suitably attired.

Our first scrimmage was that night. I sat in the Kellys' kitchen and watched my new teammates, all of them huge, arrive and troop through one by one. They were boys still, but they had the air of men. Serious. Grave. Intent. Nobody looked at me. They just said their hellos to the family and moved on out the back door into the small shed that Fred had equipped with a woodstove. I walked out there with Virgil.

The rink was lit by strings of bare light bulbs. The ice ended abruptly in shadow, and the humped rocks and spindly trees created an eerie kind of backdrop. The shed was roasting inside with a wild fire in the stove. Beneath the smell of sweat and leather was the sting of liniment and a potent mix of farts, tobacco and chewing gum. The floor was covered with a thick rubber pad and gear was strewn everywhere. The players were in varying states of undress. Long johns, hockey socks, jocks, shoulder pads. I watched as they prepared. The whipping motion of hands taping knee pads to shins. Fists pounding pads into place. Grimaces as skate laces were drawn taut. The goalies prone on the floor, lying on their bellies while other players latched the pads to the backs of their legs. The Moose were like soldiers arming themselves for battle, and I stood there holding my new gear bag in my hand, unable to move at first. The feel of their energy in that tiny shack like ordnance built to explode.

"Who's got tape?"

"Fuckin' elbow pads. Need new ones. These won't stay in place."

"Nail 'em in. You're a defenseman."

"Five bucks first goal."

"Easy money."

As I pushed into a spot on a bench beside Virgil, I could see some players glancing my way. No one said a word to me, though. Instead, they spoke among themselves. Murmurs. Grumbles. Cusses. Whenever a player was ready he'd clomp across the rubber and out the door into the chill night air. When I had drawn the laces of my new skates as tight as they would go, I wrapped a few rounds of tape around the blade of my stick and then stood to test it, leaning my weight on it and bending the shaft. Fred Kelly walked in and tossed me a jersey.

"It's mine," he said. "Wore it when I was first with the Moose."

He helped me pull it on over my shoulder pads. "Thanks," I said.

"When you get out there, Saul, I want you to take it easy. Don't jump into the play right away. Study what's going on.

Learn what you can about how these guys move, what they like to do with the puck, how they work with each other, where they're weakest, most prone to being beat. They'll tease you at first. They'll make fun of you. Some of them might even make a run at you. But take the time you need. Then, when you feel ready, join in. You got it?"

"Yeah," I said.

"Nervous?"

"Some."

"Good. Let's go."

I stood at the rink's open gate, awed by the size and speed of my teammates. I could feel the breeze they created push against my face as they whirled around the rink in warm-up. I glided out, too intimidated to move further. One of them clipped me as he passed and I twirled and spun and fell to one knee. Everybody laughed. I could feel the redness in my cheeks as I stood and began to skate on the inside, away from the boards. Virgil passed close to me.

"Skate," he hissed.

I pushed off and worked my speed up gradually, watching the team like Fred suggested. The players were powerful, but it was their sheer strength that gave most of them thrust, not their ability to skate. Their blades made that tell-tale bash against the ice when they stepped up the pace. Still, they were the fastest, most fluid players I had seen. I could see who turned better to his left, who to his right. I could see who leaned too far over his knees, to make puck-handling easy. Eventually I moved to the outside and skated with the others. But I still didn't let my speed out.

When the scrimmage started I again stood beside the boards and watched. The others shot me curious glances.

I was too intent on the game to care. The team moved the puck a lot faster and harder than I'd seen before. Their organization was tight and the game flowed up ice and down with a measured, calculated crispness. But soon I was able to read the flow, to see where the play would go and how a particular player would react to it. When I finally coasted along the right wing past Fred Kelly, he smiled at me and nodded. I turned and skated into the game.

They came at me right away. My head was at chest level for most players and they pushed me out of their way. When I tried to move ahead they held me back with their sticks. They hooked my sweater. They were unbelievably strong. They tripped me and laughed when I sprawled spread eagle on the ice. They knocked me into the boards, and pinned me there with their bulk. But there was teaching in all of it. They showed me what to expect, and I let the game flow through me. I skated loosely and waited.

Nobody would pass to me, so when the puck went into the corner and three players battled along the boards for it, I skated in and poked the puck loose with the toe of my stick. I spun on one blade, pushed off and was suddenly in open ice in front of my own goal. I stepped into my stride, crossed to the far boards and headed up ice. Virgil, on the far right wing banged his stick on the ice for a pass. I waited. When I crossed centre and approached the blue line, the biggest Moose defenseman committed. As he moved to try to check the puck from my stick, I saw Virgil angle for the hole he'd created. I snapped the puck under the defenseman's outstretched stick. Virgil had open ice. He put the puck into the low stick-side corner.

I skated to the bench and took a seat.

"Nice pass," Virgil said.

"Try that shit again, kid," the defenseman said bitterly when he cruised by. Fred Kelly grinned behind the boards.

After a whistle, I took centre for the faceoff. I lost that draw but the puck had little momentum and I snatched it and was gone in three strides. I knew the defense would try to pinch me off in the middle, so I drove straight at them. When they'd committed I leaned onto my blades and made a sharp, veering turn, the puck cradled on my stick. Our other forward poured full-steam into open ice on the other side. I hit him on the button with a drilled pass and he was away and in the clear. He failed to score, but I gobbled up the rebound from his slap shot. I was twelve feet out, and as I closed the distance to the net I deked to the right, then quickly back to the left, and lofted the puck up under the crossbar. The defense banged their sticks on the ice in frustration.

As I skated back to the bench again, the whole team was staring at me. Virgil slapped my shin pads with his stick. The rest stayed where they were and as I slumped down on the bench there were some low mutters of appreciation.

It got harder after that. Every time I touched the puck, someone was on me. They used their size to take the ice away from me. They forced me to the boards and held me there with their weight and bulk. They slammed their sticks on the shaft of mine or they just reached in with their strength and lifted the blade of my stick off the ice. They made me work harder than I had ever had to work. For a while they completely restricted my movement and I grew frustrated and angry. They gave catcalls when I sat on the bench and hooted when my progress was stalled anywhere on the ice. My body hurt. But my pride hurt more.

Eventually, it made me better. Instead of following the play, where I could be bashed and bothered, I moved into open ice, and they would not follow me away from the flow. From there I could ratchet up my speed. I dashed into the play and they couldn't hit me or hold me because they couldn't catch me. I whirled and danced and darted with the puck. I didn't score another goal but I made three or four pinpoint passes that resulted in goals. I also didn't take another hit. There was no fear in me. There was no anxiety. There was only the magic of the game.

When the whistle blew the team gathered at the boards nearest the shack. They leaned on their sticks and heaved great clouds of breath into the bitter cold. Fred Kelly tapped a clipboard against his thigh and looked over to where I stood by the net, uncertain about what to do or where to go. Finally, Virgil banged his stick on the ice and stepped aside to make room for me. Everyone else shunted over. I skated slowly to them and stepped into that empty space and Fred began to talk. He highlighted things he wanted us all to pay attention to. He spoke to specific players about specific plays. When he got to me he just smiled.

"Welcome to the Moose," he said.

Virgil thumped me on the back and they all rattled the blades of their sticks on the ice and we thumped across the snow to the shack.

We sat in the blistering heat created by that woodstove, towels wrapped around our necks, drops of sweat making a marsh on the thick rubber mat. My teammates sucked greedily at pop and water. Here and there someone fired up a cigarette. Skates and other gear dropped to the floor. They sat in varying degrees of undress. Boys, almost men, the feel of them languid, loose and easy now. Virgil handed me a soda and I lifted the bottle and took a long draught. It felt and tasted magnificent. When I set it down under the bench and sat up to peel my jersey off, they raised their own bottles to me silently and drank. No one said a word. They didn't have to. I stripped off my jersey and sat there breathing in the atmosphere of that small wooden shack. I was a Moose.

————— 26

The Moose travelled to games in a pair of broken-down vans that Virgil worked his mechanical magic on to keep running. Fred's shifts at work made it almost impossible for him to go with us as our coach so Virgil did that as well as captain the team. Our gear was stacked on the roof. We were crushed together, except for Virgil, who did the driving, and the front-seat passenger. We'd doze off to the smell of feet and sour breath and the sounds of snoring on those long, pitch-black northern drives, some of them three hundred miles or more. We existed on fruit, chocolate bars and sandwiches prepared for us by someone's mother or girlfriend. It was my job as the rookie to clear out the van at every stop. We'd leave on Friday night, right after the work whistles blew at the mills or the mines. In the fading light of the sun we'd follow the dim, humped white of the snowdrifts at the road's shoulder into the northern bush.

Because I was the smallest one on the team, I always found myself scrunched between two larger players. They'd cut cards to see who got to sit beside me: I took up less space, so there was more room for those on either side to get comfortable. Often, while the others were sleeping, I'd look out the window and watch the land flow by. Some nights there would be a moon, and the shadows it created were spectacular. Trees became many-armed creatures looming across the road. Lakes were shining phosphorescent platters. Ridges and scarps were fortresses capped with snow. Rivers were serpentine swaths of a deeper black. I loved every inch of it. I'd largely given up mourning the loss of my early life, those days on the land with my family. But the sadness filled me at times as we drove through the night.

Whether our destination was Gull River, Longlac, Red Rock, Whitesand or Ginoogaming, we were welcomed into the community and billeted with families who took good care of us. Sometimes five or six players would hunker in with a family of twelve in a small clapboard reserve house, bodies sprawled around the woodstove or laid out in rows across the main room. They served us rabbit, beaver and moose. When the time came to play, we'd all tramp through the snow to the rinks. Sometimes we played on rivers, or lakes or ponds. More often the rinks had been set up behind the band office or community centre. There would always be a wooden shack that both teams shared to suit up in. Those shacks were incredible. Lit by the brightest of light bulbs and warmed by stoves with a chimney pipe that stuck up through a hole in the roof, they had gouged plywood floors that you could see the ground through. The benches had to be replaced every year, because someone always made off with the benches from the year prior to use for firewood. When we clomped down the plywood ramps onto the ice, our skates sounded like thunder rolling across the vast whiteness. The rinks were much the same wherever we went. Wooden boards braced by two-by-fours.

Chicken wire stretched across each end behind the nets. Three or four strings of light bulbs draped across the blue lines and centre ice, with maybe another yard light mounted on a hydro pole. Sometimes there were bleachers, but for the most part the crowds stood shoulder to shoulder around the perimeter, ducking when the puck flew over the boards. But the ice was always smooth and well tended. Each host community took great care to prepare it. People loved the game. It might be thirty below with a wind whipping across the surface of the rink and stinging their eyes, but they would stand there and stamp their feet and lean closer to each other like penguins. They'd stand for the length of the game, then scurry into the community hall or the nearest house to warm before the next game started. They were the hardiest and most devoted fans you could ever wish for. We played our hearts out for them.

Those games were spirited contests and gruelling physical feats. The white people had denied us the privilege of indoor arenas, the comfort of heated dressing rooms, concession stands, glassed rinks, scoreboards and even a players' bench. We stood behind the boards, stamping our skates in the snow to keep our feet warm. In the coldest weather we took turns heading to the shack for warmth, leaving just six players from each side on the ice. The goalies would take turns too. But we played each game out. No game was ever called because of weather. We skated through blizzards, deep Arctic freezes and sudden thaws that turned the ice to butter. The game brought us together in a way that nothing else could, and players and fans alike huddled against whatever winter threw at us. We celebrated every goal, every hit, every pass. Sometimes there were fights as there are so often in the game, but they were never bitter, never carried on beyond the next faceoff. We came from nations of warriors, and the sudden flinging down of sticks and gloves, the wild punches and wrestling were extensions of that identity. A fight would end and both players would shake hands. The crowd would cheer and clap and stamp their feet, and the game would carry on.

Everywhere we went I was greeted with laughter because I was so young and so small. We played five games at the end of that first winter. At the beginning of each game I hung back as Fred Kelly had asked me to do. But when I had seen enough, I jumped in and the laughter died away. The higher level of play with these bigger and better teams did not stall me. Instead, it pushed me to greater heights. By the end of that first winter, I was an essential part of the Moose.

"Our secret weapon," Buddy Black Wolf said.

"A bag of antlers," was how Ervin Ear described me. "But fast."

_____ 27

Every reserve in the North had a team. Indian boys grew up in those communities knowing that when they got old enough and good enough they could wear the sweaters of their home reserve. Whenever I saw younger kids racing around in decrepit skates with broken sticks, chasing a ball or a sawed-off tin can filled with dirt, I remembered horse turds and hockey sticks stuffed in a snowbank and I smiled. The teams were their communities' pride and joy. We paid about ten dollars each to play those tournaments and the winner team took home a small purse. Mostly you won enough to cover the gas to get you home and people were happy with that. The first game was held late Friday night as soon as the first teams arrived, and games ran all day Saturday. The championship game was early enough on the Sunday morning to allow everyone time to get home and be ready for work the next day. Everybody stayed to watch the final outcome. Everyone wanted to be a part of the celebration at the end. We lived for the crush of bodies and the yelling and the clapping and the tumult that greeted the champions regardless of who won.

The first part of our journey home was raucous. We replayed every shift, every pass, goal and rush. We teased each other over losing the puck or taking a hit. We laughed at lapses in thinking or sudden misadventures. We praised each other for things well done. When we finally fell asleep it was to dreams of hockey. It was the same for every team, I believe. We came together every weekend with the same anticipation, waiting for the release that happened when our skate blades hit the ice. The rink was the place where our dreams came to life.

It couldn't really be called a league. But there was a network of reserve communities flung across the North and each team captain took it as his responsibility to get the word out before freeze-up about when his community would host its tournament. The news travelled by moccasin telegraph. The spring, summer and fall were the times for players to train, to run, to lift weights and get their bodies ready for the new season to come.

We were hockey gypsies, heading down another gravel road every weekend, plowing into the heart of that magnificent northern landscape. We never gave a thought to being deprived as we travelled, to being shut out of the regular league system. We never gave a thought to being Indian. Different. We only thought of the game and the brotherhood that bound us together off the ice, in the van, on the plank floors of reservation houses, in the truck stop diners where if we'd won we had a little to splurge on a burger and soup before we hit the road again. Small joys. All of them tied together, entwined to form an experience we would not have traded for any other. We were a league of nomads, mad for the game, mad for the road, mad for ice and snow, an Arctic wind on our faces and a frozen puck on the blade of our sticks.

Fred and Martha Kelly were good to me. They didn't try to be parents. They settled for being friends, and Virgil and I grew close. He was my greatest ally. I'd never done homework before or had teachers pay any attention to me. The idea of school as a process of grades and expectations was new and frightening. Virgil sat up late with me and helped me with my lessons. He taught me how to understand school, how to present myself in class, how to fit in with the other kids, and tips and tricks to help me learn faster. School became a pleasure with his help. At home I was asked to help out with household chores. I'd been trained to work at St. Jerome's. Anything the Kellys asked me to do, I did smartly and well. The first time they thanked me for my efforts I had no words. Because of their own experience with St. Germ's, they understood. Home life became an easy thing and I got comfortable quickly.

My second winter in Manitouwadge, I took to rising early just as I did at St. Jerome's, clearing the ice and then practicing until it was time to leave for school. I was almost fifteen. Virgil would join me on the ice when he had a later shift at the mine. I would practice escaping his clutches and holds and the snare of his stick as he leaned into me, using his size and girth to slow me down. He was fast for a big man. By that second winter I had almost reached my full height and size, five-foot-nine and one hundred and forty pounds. So I was still small. Virgil had showed me how to work with weights the summer before, and I was lean and wiry. Still, he outweighed me by almost seventy pounds.

"Don't get caught along the boards. Use the ice. Use as much as they give you," he'd say. "Use your speed to give yourself more."

During our team practices Fred would sometimes send me out against three of the other players. They would chase me, hit me, grab me. Every time I touched the puck in those sessions, a body was there. Every time I turned, someone was right up against me. It took a lot of work to find my rhythm under this kind of pressure, but I did it. Those three-on-ones taught me to activate my vision as if it had a switch. When the bumping and the holding impeded me, I'd coast, let the game go, watch it flow around me, just breathing until the vision descended like a cloud of light again. I would see the ice, the players, the destination of the puck as clearly as if the action were on a movie screen. But I had to call my vision forward with emotion; with longing for that purity of motion, the freedom that the game gave me.

"You go somewhere when you're on the ice," Virgil said to me after one practice. "It's like watching you walk into a secret place that no one else knows how to get to."

28

We won ten out of the fifteen tournaments we played that second year. We scored goals by the bucketful. Fred Kelly called us "a war party on skates." He usually put me out on each of our three lines. That meant I played almost forty minutes of every game, but I never lost focus. None of the other players on the team complained. How could they? They would find themselves with the puck suddenly appearing on their stick out of nowhere. They learned to head for open ice at every opportunity. We became a team of skilled passers. Instead of letting the puck lead us around by the nose, as so many other teams did, the Moose began to go where the puck wasn't, trusting that a team-mate would send it there, and they would pick it up with another golden chance to score.

Father Leboutilier showed up at a game in Pic River that winter. It was late November, and we'd been playing for a month already. I didn't notice him in the crowd, but when we clumped up the ramp to the shack he called to me from the side. I was surprised to see him. He looked different in his civilian clothes. Not like a priest at all. He smiled as if he knew what I was thinking. After I had changed I met him by the boards, and we walked together to his old battered car. We talked about the game and I settled into the remembered feeling of our friendship.

"You make the other players better, Saul," he said.

"They make me work harder too."

"That's what I hoped when I sent you to the Kellys. That the game would lift you higher."

"They treat me good."

"The Kellys?"

"And the Moose. The people around the circuit. It feels great."

We wound our way along the highway and back toward the community hall. "I hope I was able to help you when you were with us at the school," he said.

"You did," I said.

"I'm proud of you, Saul." We were parked in the hall's lot by then and he grabbed me and pulled me across the seat to hold me close. I could hear his breathing. When he let me go I could feel his eyes on me. "I don't know when I will see you again."

"I know," I said.

"You're free now, Saul. Free to let the game take you where it will."

I got out without another word and stood in the snow and watched his old car disappear around the bend. His leaving was an ache that stayed with me for days. I would never see him again.

29

By February of that year, the Northern winter was at its deepest. The Moose kept winning and news of our success travelled beyond the confines of the reservation circuit. We were playing at a tournament in Longlac when Virgil poked me in the ribs with his stick as we stood by the boards.

"White guys," he said. They stood behind the chicken wire at the end of the rink, far away from the regular crowd. Six of them. They wore identical team jackets and they were big, but clearly nervous to be on the reserve.

"What are they doing here?" I asked.

"Gonna find out," Virgil said.

After the game, I left the shack to find Virgil talking to them, his arms crossed over his chest. When he saw me he waved me over.

"These guys wanna play us," he said. "Exhibition game. In Kapuskasing."

"You play a hell of a game," the tallest one said. "Your team's too good for these other guys here."

"We do okay," I said.

"The thing is, we wonder if you can win at another level. Against us. We want to challenge you."

Virgil hooked a thumb at me and the two of us moved off to the side,

They were from the Kapuskasing Chiefs, a Senior A team comprised of mill and mine workers. They played in the Northern Hockey Association against teams from Schreiber, Terrace, Geraldton, Marathon and Hearst. They were good—more than good—and the town of Kapuskasing was proud of them.

"One game," Virgil said. "They were league champions last year. I figure, why not?"

"We never played in town before," I said.

"Rink's a rink."

"Maybe," I said, remembering White River.

"These Kapuskasing guys would give us a good game," Virgil said

"We already play good games."

"Yeah. We do. But these other teams aren't exactly pushing us. Maybe we could be even better. There's only one way to find out."

We stared at each other. I could see the hunger in him. He wanted this game.

"We'll pay your gas. Give you food money," the tall player called over to us. "It'd be worth it to us."

"Hear that, Saul? Can't get a better deal than that."

"I don't want to play in town. I did that. It was no good."

"You weren't a Moose then." Virgil looked at me hard. "If the other guys on the team want to do it, we're going. That's how it's gonna be."

They'd decided before we went on the ice for our next game. The idea of the challenge excited my teammates and nothing I said could curb their enthusiasm. All they could think about was an indoor arena with manufactured ice and a dressing room we wouldn't need to share and showers and toilets. So the game was booked and we began to practice harder than ever before. Fred Kelly was determined to ice a competitive squad and he drove us to excel. We did the same passing drills over and over again. He worked us on clearing the puck from our own end, freeing it in the corner for faceoffs and using the sixty feet between blue lines to gather momentum and arrange ourselves for attack. The players changed. Our practices, usually marked by good-natured yelps and shouts, became solemn, with everyone bearing down. The silence was disturbing.

"We're not the same team," I said to Virgil one night.

"What's the problem with that? We're better."

"It doesn't feel better."

"You're just scared."

"I'm not scared. I just want it back the way it used to be."

"We've never had a chance to be great before."

"We were great."

"Against teams that couldn't push us."

"Great's great."

"Easy enough for you to say, Saul. But none of us have your gift. Think about us guys. Think about how much we'd like a shot at playing at a higher level. Think about that."

So I did. In the end that was the only reason I decided to skate against Kapuskasing. I didn't want the Moose to fail. I didn't want them coming back defeated, bearing the memory of a battle they'd never had a chance to win. If there was anything that I could do to prevent that I would. I'd bring my best game. I would bring my entire focus. I'd bring every ounce of my will. My team needed me to play my best and that's the only reason I decided to play that game.

———— 30

The Kapuskasing arena was new. The town had spent a lot of money on it and when we walked into the lobby the first thing we saw were glass cabinets along the walls filled with trophies and photographs. It was like a shrine to their home team. We stood there with our gear bags in our hands, studying the display. There were no awards in our bush league. The winners were celebrated with feasts and parties but there was no money for trophies. It was Virgil who finally broke off our reverie and led us to the dressing room.

"Shiny things," he said. "You guys are like a bunch of crows."

The dressing room was warm and well lit. Each player had a small cubicle and we all had room to sprawl out and stretch on the floor while we dressed. I could see the nerves working on the Moose. These were Indian boys. They may have been lumberjacks and mine workers when they weren't playing the game, but concrete arenas and carpeted dressing rooms intimidated them. Fred Kelly hadn't been able to make the trip. That unnerved them even more. Because of the Chiefs' regular league schedule, the game could only be booked in mid-week and no one could pick up Fred's shifts at the mine. We'd made the nearly three-hundred-mile trip in a strange, nervous quiet. Virgil did his best to assure the team that he had Fred's game plan memorized, but my teammates were still anxious. None of them said a thing, and the quiet of our preparations was unnerving. We could hear the noisy crowd wending its way along the corridor and up into the seats. It sounded like a few thousand people. Their voices were shrill and excited. There was a knock at the door, and Virgil stumped over to answer it.

"Need your lineup card," someone said.

"Our what?" Virgil asked.

"Your lineup card. For the refs and the announcer."

"We don't got one."

"You need one."

I took a few minutes to write our names and numbers on a card. When I handed it to the older man who stood waiting, the man looked at it and smiled. "You got some pretty weird names here," he said. "Indian Horse. Black Wolf. Ear. You're kidding, right?"

Virgil just looked at him steadily.

When we were ready, we stood up, waiting for someone to make the first move. "It's just an exhibition game," Virgil said. "It's just another game so don't make it bigger in your heads. Play it like you always do. Be Moose. Be Indians."

He led us to the ice. The building was like a great cavern. Flags and pennants hung from the rafters. The bright lights gave the ice the look of cotton. The red and blue lines were stark against it. The goalposts glared from each end and behind them the sparkling glass reached tall above the boards. The seats stretched back to form a shallow bowl around the rink, and the place was packed. As soon as we pushed out onto the ice the crowd began to shout at us. People laughed when they saw me, and I could hear them heckle as I skated around to loosen up.

"Thirteen must be the mascot!"

"No, no. That's papoose. Thirteen's their papoose!"

"Hey, thirteen! You got a note from your mom to play?"

The announcer cut in to introduce our lineup. We'd never heard our names over a loudspeaker before, and our guys raised their heads to listen. The crowd reacted whenever he read out a particularly Indian-sounding name, shouting out jibes and taunts. When the Chiefs skated out onto the ice, the people in the stands rose and erupted in foot stomping, hand clapping, whistles and cheers. The Chiefs circled in their end. They skated really well in their flashy uniforms and gear. We went through our warm-ups and gathered on our bench to prepare.

"Just like we always do," Virgil said. "If my dad was here, he'd be telling you the same thing. We just need to play our game. Our game. No matter what."

I was astonished at the skill and precision of the Chiefs. They were awesome to watch. I'd never seen a team that good play in person. Everybody knew exactly where the others were at all times, and passes that seemed aimed for open ice were gobbled up by their players streaking into it. They seemed programmed to aim for our net and they worked the puck effortlessly back and forth. They potted four goals against us in the first eight minutes. I hung back and watched them as I usually did. The score was five to nothing before I got that feeling of space behind my eyes, the clarity I was so familiar with. I signalled to Virgil, who was taking a breather near the gate to our bench, and he nodded.

"Little Chief," he yelled and pounded on the boards. On his next pass Stu Little Chief headed for the bench. When he was three feet away I hurtled over the boards and into the game.

As soon as my skates hit the ice I knew exactly what to do. I burst down the right side and followed the puck deep into their end. Their defenseman scooped the puck off the boards and cut behind their net. The rest of them banked like fighter planes. That's what I was counting on. I could see that the Chiefs' first pass would be a hard flat one to their other defender halfway to the blue line. From there it was supposed to go across ice behind our retreating forwards, to their left-winger, who would tap it directly into open ice. Their centre would pick it up at full speed and head up ice. But they never got that chance. I was out of the defenseman's range of vision, and when he sent out the first pass I cut in off the wing, where I coasted. I was blazing when the cross-ice pass was made and I snared it at their blue line. I heard the defenders yelp and they both jumped up to counter. I turned hard on the outside edge of my blades, pulled the puck around on my backhand and cut straight across in front of them. Fast. They had to come together, and when they did I cut the other way and swept into clear ice near the far faceoff circle. They couldn't catch me. I straightened up fifteen feet in front of the net, dipped my shoulders, wriggled my hips and changed direction three times before lifting the puck over the sprawled goalie. Five to one.

indian horse

I barely went to the bench after that. The only rest I got was between periods, and by the time we came out for the final frame it was five to four for the Chiefs. By then they were keying on me, which opened up the ice for the rest of our guys. But they were a strong and disciplined team. Even when two of them took me out against the boards the other three skaters maintained control of their territory. My teammates played hard, but the experience of the Kapuskasing kept us at bay. They knew how to play puck control and they iced the puck at lot to force faceoffs. Time was wearing down. My energy began to flag. I signalled to Virgil with seven minutes left and took a seat on the bench. I squirted water over my head from a plastic bottle and wiped it off with a towel. The Chiefs and their crowd could smell victory, and the noise was tremendous. None of us had ever been in such a raucous atmosphere. When our players came to the bench I could see fear on their faces. The tension was huge. This loss would be enormous and I closed my eyes and breathed, drawing all my energy to a sharp point of focus. I felt lifted suddenly, borne upward and out of my tired body, and the air was suddenly clearer in my lungs. I waved a glove at a passing player and he whirled to the bench and I was back into the flow of the game. I stole the puck off a Chief player's stick at their blue line and whirled and snapped a bullet of a pass right onto Virgil's stick. The goalie slid across the crease with his pads stacked together. Virgil calmly lifted the puck over him. Tie game.

Five minutes left, and I was flying now. Every time the Chiefs tried a rush I broke it up. Every time they worked to organize themselves I would rag the puck in a wild game of keep-away until their attack fizzled. The crowd shouted at them to hit me but I was too fast. I spun and danced and looped-the-loop like a daredevil. I skated like I had never skated before. I made seemingly impossible passes. I made moves that made the crowd roar. Then, with less than a minute remaining, I poke-checked the puck off a Chief defenseman's stick. It squirted out into the open and I flashed past him and scooped it up with one hand on my stick. I pumped hard with the other and sped across centre ice. The crowd stood and yelled at their team to stop me. I raised my eyes to look ahead. Their goalie was backing slowly toward the net. The Moose were all yelling from our bench, and that's when time slowed. I could hear the slice of my blades. I could hear my own breathing. I zoomed across the blue line but everything was all cottony and slow. The puck was pushed out ahead of me on the toe of the blade of my stick.

My shoulders rolled as I sped in on goal. I could see the goalie squinting through the cage of his mask. When I was a dozen feet away I dropped one shoulder in a broad feint. He didn't move. I faked a wrist shot. At the last second I turned my stick and pulled the puck back in, at the same time turning sharply so I faced back up ice. The goalie had moved across the net with me. I saw Stu Little Chief skating in all alone on the opposite side of the net and I hit him on the button with a hard pass. All he had to do was tap it into the empty side of the goal. I didn't see the Chiefs defenseman coming. He hit me hard and I crashed into the boards. When I clambered to one knee the Moose piled on top of me. I was pummelled and punched in joy and by the time we got untangled the ice was littered with debris. The crowd was standing and cheering, and as I skated to our bench with thirty seconds left in the game they cheered even louder. The ice crew cleared up the mess and I sat on the bench as our guys controlled the puck after the faceoff. The players on the bench stood as the time clicked away and then erupted over the boards when the klaxon sounded. I was too tired to move.

Finally, the Chiefs lined up to shake our hands and I made my way off the bench to join the ceremony. One by one they gripped my hand and nodded. The crowd kept up their applause. We skated to our bench and were headed towards the dressing room when someone stopped me at the exit and told me I was the game's first star. I didn't understand.

"The first star," Virgil said. "You know? Three stars like *Hockey Night in Canada*?"

"I'm not going back out there."

"Have to. It's tradition."

"I don't know if I like that tradition," I said.

"Guess you better start to if you're gonna play like that."

Then the announcer's voice boomed out across the arena. "Introducing the game's three stars. Your first star, from the Manitouwadge Moose, number thirteen, Saul Indian Horse. Indian Horse."

I expected boos to rain down. But when I coasted out to take a turn around centre ice, the applause and stamping feet sounded like thunder rolling around the arena. I looked up and everybody was standing and when I raised my stick in appreciation they cheered even louder. I skated to the bench and Virgil was grinning at me.

"Better'n a fricking trophy any time, eh?" he said.

"It'll do," I said and grinned. "Can we go home now?"

31 ———

That game with the Kapuskasing Chiefs took us out of our shelter. Word got out about the Indian team that had beat the Senior A champions, and everyone wanted to play us. I wasn't keen and Fred shared my apprehension, but Virgil and the others were determined to take up the challenge.

"They think it's their game," I said. "I found that out at the school."

Virgil frowned. "They play the game for the same reason we do. For the feeling. Far as I know, no one owns that."

"They think they do."

"Yeah. Well. We'll see."

Instead of our regular northern trips, we began travelling to towns dotted all along the Trans-Canada Highway, places we'd heard of or passed through but never had a reason to stop in before. There were teams everywhere, all of them eager to take on the upstart Indians from Manitouwadge. We lost some games and we won our share, but there was less joy in the trips. A motel in Timmins was less inviting than our regular billets in Batchewana. The air in those arenas didn't move. You couldn't feel the wind off the lake cutting across the blue line or follow a honking flock of geese across the sky. There were no Indian kids chasing after the pucks that got flipped over the boards into the snow; no brown fingers clutching the chicken wire behind the net. Zambonis replaced the gangs of people in gumboots and mackinaws hosing down the ice. Now the norm was rows of red seats, electronic scoreboards, junk food in Styrofoam boxes, and the jagged sound of English in the taunts and put-downs from the crowds.

"This ice is crap," I complained to Virgil. "On outdoor ice you really gotta know how to skate."

"It's arena ice," he said. "Same everywhere."

"That's what I mean. The ice in Heron Bay was rough where the wind cut through the black spruce and made ripples and ridges. It was uneven in Ginoogaming because the ground slanted up from one end. We had to know that. Had to use it in our game."

"This makes it easier."

"Easier ain't better. It's just easier."

We played almost every week in another town. The games were always events, mostly because people were curious to see if Indians could really skate, if we could play the game right. Although I didn't want to be there, I took it as my personal responsibility to show them. The white players tried to rough me up but I used my speed to leave them behind me. They speared me, elbowed me, slashed me, head-butted me, but I always found the open ice I needed to make another play, to create magic out of mayhem. The rest of the Moose fought for me. I could shrug off a cheap hit in favour of a better opportunity, but my teammates resented the way I was treated. They resented the cold, inhospitable way we were all treated. For them, the game had always been gentlemanly; rough and hard for certain, but clean, and the reserve teams and the communities that spawned them had been like family. Now there were out-and-out brawls. Once, when I got laid out after a crushing hit from behind, they streamed off our bench and the fight that ensued was horrific. It took the referees a full twenty minutes to get things calmed down. Once the penalties were sorted out, both teams were left with four forwards, a pair of defensemen and a goalie. The crowd was rabid. Garbage rained down on us. A group of them pissed and shat in our dressing room. The tires were slashed on the vans. No one spoke after that game, which we lost by two goals. My teammates carried that resentment with them, and the games we played after were tougher and harder, more bitterly fought, and once, in Hearst, when things again got out of control and blood spewed in an epic team fight in the third period, they refused to line up for the handshakes at the end of the game. They grew vengeful and no cheap shot went unpaid with fists. It saddened me. The Moose went from jubilant boys to hard, taciturn men in no time at all. But as long as we kept winning our share, none of them ventured a suggestion that we return to the way it had been.

It drove me to even deeper focus. I worked deliberately at getting that keen sense of vision to alight on me faster. I wanted to spare my team the indignity of a brawl. I wanted to keep the spirit of the game instilled in them and let them play with the freedom and abandon they once had. So I worked hard at learning to connect to that vision. It started to take me less and less time to read those teams. The players had all grown up the same way, with the same kind of coaching, the same perceptions of the game. Their ideas of flow and movement were restricted by the predictable nature of their coaching, and they seldom took the risk of breaking out of the standard mode of play. I saw that and took advantage of it. Soon we'd left the bush circuit behind altogether and we were invited to play in big-money tournaments everywhere. We earned enough our first winter out to buy new uniforms. Everyone was excited.

Then we ran into the black heart of northern Ontario in the 1960s and we were hated. Hated. There's no other word for it. The Moose came out of the bush as a team that wanted to prove itself against the best competition around. We arrived in those towns as hockey players expecting to play a square game, stick to stick, end to end, fair and equal. But they only ever saw us as Indians. They only ever saw brown faces where white ones should have been. We were an unwelcome entity in their midst. And when we won it only made things worse.

Chapleau was a mill town east of Wawa, and the tournament there drew teams from as far away as Timmins and Sudbury. A lot of pride was on the line. The games were scrappy and tough and it took everything we had to wrest the championship game from the Sault Ste. Marie team. But we did it. It was a long drive back to Manitouwadge and the boys all had to work the next day, so we decided to spend some of our winnings on a meal in Devon, a small town outside of Chapleau. There wasn't much to the place, but the café in a hotel looked okay. When we walked through the door, we could see another door that led to a bar. Whenever the door swung open, we could hear the sound of a jukebox and the laughter of men. We were the only ones in the café. We took four tables by the window overlooking the street. The waitress took our orders and we were recounting the game highlights and laughing when a man entered. He took a long look at us before retreating into the bar. None of us gave it a thought.

Then the music from the jukebox stopped.

I looked up to see a line of men entering the café from the bar. They were working men, big and strong-looking with stern faces. Several of them sat on stools and spun around on them to face us. The rest stood around our tables. There were eight of them.

"You boys got kinda big for the britches," a swarthy, tall man said and leaned one hand on the table where Virgil and I sat.

"No idea what you mean," Virgil said. He kept his face neutral.

"Well, you win a little hockey tournament and then you think you got the right to come in here and eat like white people," the man said.

"We're only here to eat. We didn't set out to copy anybody," Virgil said.

"Don't get cute with me boy."

Virgil pushed his chair back and stood up. "Boy?" he asked. "How big do they grow men where you come from?"

The man sneered. "Plenty bigger'n you."

"Just what the hell do you want?"

"Well, the thing is, you gotta earn the right to eat here."

"We pay just like everybody else."

"We don't eat with Indians."

"I don't recall asking you to join us," Virgil said.

The man smiled. Then he reached out and clamped a hand on Virgil's shoulder. "It's not your place to ask us anything. You wanna eat here you gotta fight for it."

"What are you talking about?"

"Well, whenever we get Indians uppity enough to wanna eat here we take them outside to a little place in the alley out back we call Moccasin Square Garden. You walk back in here from the Garden and you can eat all you want. So we're gonna march you out there one at a time. See who's man enough to make it back."

"Sounds fun." Virgil reached down and took a drink of water, then placed the glass back on the table.

"You first," the man said to him.

"Save my spot, Saul. I'll be right back."

The line of men walked Virgil out and three more stepped from the door of the bar to block our passage. They had axe handles in their hands. We sat there in shock, not knowing what to do. The waitress and the cook stood together in the kitchen, murmuring to each other. There was the sound of slushy traffic from the street. A police car slid by and we flicked looks at each other. The team sat ramrod straight in our chairs.

They walked Virgil back in. He was bloody around the mouth and there was a cut on his temple. He wiped his mouth with the back of his hand as he sat down and stared at his hands, which he'd folded on the table. Then they walked another of us out. For the next twenty minutes they came in and took one member of the Moose after another. Each time they brought someone back the smell of urine got stronger. When only I was left, the tall man leaned on our table.

"You play a hell of game, little star," he said. "That and the fact that you're a kid gives you a pass. But remember your place. Next time, somewheres else, you might not get so lucky."

He blew a kiss to everyone at our table and then turned and walked away. The other men strode out behind him. As they entered the bar the jukebox jumped back to life we heard a lot of laughter and the clinking of glasses. I sat there looking around at my teammates' faces. None of them moved. They were all staring at the table in front of them. They'd been beaten. Not severely. They weren't injured enough to require a hospital but they were cut and hurt, and I could feel their brokenness. Virgil cleared his throat and stood up.

"Let's go," he said.

We filed out silently and climbed into the van. Virgil motioned for me to join him in the front seat. We pulled out into the street and found the highway again. No one said a word. The smell of urine and spit was high in the air. Someone lit a cigarette and the acrid bite of the smoke was a relief. Virgil drove steadily, west along the road that would take us home. Darkness fell. We drove in silence. There was no sound for miles except the hum of the wheels beneath us. We'd driven for hours before Virgil spoke. When he did it was only five words. Five words that scared me and angered me at the same time.

"They pissed on us, Saul."

The miles flew by and now and then we could hear a cough from the back of the van and the rustle of bodies trying to sleep. As we passed White River around midnight, he told me what had happened.

"When I got out back they circled me. The first one came at me and we got into it. But all he did was push me back and someone else grabbed me and spun me around and I got punched in the face. Then someone else grabbed me and gave me another shot. They pushed me all around that circle, punching and kicking and when I fell to the ground, dizzy, one of them stood over me and pissed on me. It was the same for all of us."

I sat there without a clue about what to say. After a few more miles he spoke again.

"But you know what the scariest thing was, Saul? There was no yelling, no cussing, no nothing. They did it silently. Like it was an everyday thing. I never knew people could be that cold."

"They hate us because we won?" I asked finally.

"They hate us because we're skins."

"We didn't do anything."

"We crossed a line. Their line. They figure they got the right to make us pay for that."

"Do they?"

"I don't know," he said. "Sometimes I think so."

"Virgil?"

"Yeah?"

"I won't say nothing."

"Good," he said. "None of us will."

And we never did. But there were moments when you'd catch another boy's eye and know that you were both thinking about it. Everything was contained in that glance. All the hurt. All the shame. All the rage. The white people thought it was their game. They thought it was their world.

32 ———

I started to notice things after that. I started to see a line in every arena we played in. It showed itself as a stretch of empty seats that separated the Indian fans from the white ones. Police were stationed at the separate entrance they shunted our people through. I saw that a lot of players on the opposing teams would not remove their hockey gloves to shake our hands after a game. Some of them didn't even leave the bench. When I mentioned it to Virgil, he scowled. "White ice, white players," he said. "Honky Night in Canada."

The Moose were invited to play in a town called Espanola. It was a long drive, but their team, the Lumber Kings, were repeat champions. Several former members had graduated to Major Junior A and a handful had even gone on to play in the National Hockey League. They were a team with a pedigree, and only the best teams got invited to Espanola's annual tournament. The tournament had never had a Native team before, and despite some misgivings Virgil convinced us to make the trip.

"We win this thing and we've got enough for a down payment on a team bus," he said. "Let's show them that we can do it."

The Moose were a known team by then, and when we piled out of our vans at the arena in Espanola, I could feel the eyes on us.

"Which one's the whiz kid?" I heard someone ask.

"Gotta be the big guy."

"Nah. I bet he's the tall one, with the big hands."

As we skated onto the ice for our game against the North Bay Nuggets, the crowd booed us. When our lineup was introduced, they knew suddenly where to direct their energy.

"Hey, Indian Horse! Thirteen's gonna be real unlucky for you!"

"You guys are gonna need an Indian hearse to get outta here!"

"We're taking your scalps, Chief!"

Once we settled on our bench, Virgil looked at me and grinned, trying to keep his spirits up. "They warmed up to you real fast," he said. "The Indian hearse thing was pretty good."

The North Bay team was exciting to watch. You could tell that they were well coached by the disciplined way they moved the puck. Fred Kelly seldom made a road trip because of his work schedule, and I found myself wishing for his presence right then. No one on the North Bay team took unnecessary chances. They played the game efficiently, and nobody held on to the puck for long. I was impressed as I studied their game. They weren't afraid to halt the flow and turn their rush back when it wasn't shaping up. Their defense was solid, if unspectacular. They were the stay-at-home variety who kept their heads and passed cleanly. The Nuggets could really skate too. Our guys looked awkward compared to them. Not long into the game they scored a pair of goals on us.

Virgil slumped down beside me on the bench and elbowed me in the ribs.

"You scared of these guys or what?" he asked.

"They're good."

"Yeah, well, anytime you feel like helping out."

I nodded. I watched a few minutes longer, and when one of their rushes broke down at our blue line and they turned the puck back to their trailing defenseman, I had the knowledge I needed. I raised my stick as Virgil skated by. He turned to the bench immediately and I leaped over the boards.

I burst in across our blue line to a tangle along the boards and tapped the puck loose. It skimmed out to one of their players, and I was on him in a flash. There was no sound from my skates so I surprised him. He flipped a hurried pass into the middle. Our defense ate it up and we started up ice. When they assembled to stave off our attack, I turned and skated as fast as I could along the right wing, ignoring the puck. I saw their defense tighten nervously as I flew across centre ice. They moved toward me but I cut hard back toward the play, passing our rushing left-winger in a blur. He left the puck for me, and I scooped it and flew across our blue line in a long sweeping turn. I could feel the air whip by my face, and my jersey flapped. The crowd was on their feet. I'd never skated so fast. When I met their forwards coming back toward me, I did a crazy loop-the-loop around their centre and another one in the opposite direction by their left-winger. I pulled the defense to me again as I crossed the blue line and made a nifty drop pass between my legs. Joe Eagle Chief, our right-winger, picked it up all alone and scored on a wrist shot. I'd never heard such noise—cheers mixed with boos and a crazed stomping of feet. A flurry of empty cups landed on the ice as I skated to the bench.

"They play clean, but high speed disrupts them," I huffed to Virgil.

He thumped me on the back, then whispered to our guys along the bench. From then on, we picked up the intensity on every shift. I played forty minutes of that game. I was drenched in sweat. My gear felt like it weighed a thousand pounds. I scored four times and we won it going away, seven to four. Half of their team refused to come out for the handshake.

When we returned the next morning to play the Owen Sound Clippers, the arena was packed. Like before, the crowd was noisy. The Clippers were a hard-skating, work-manlike team, known for their toughness. They were the biggest team we'd ever faced too, and when I lined up for the faceoff against their number one centre he loomed over me.

"Watch your head, squirt," he said.

Maybe I should have registered those words as ominous. Maybe I should have been able to read what was coming, discerned intent from the vicious way he slapped my stick before the puck was dropped. But I didn't. What tipped me off first was the hard cross-check I took across the back when I went into the corner after the puck. It was so hard I lost my footing and tumbled into the boards. I heard laughter from the seats. My helmet had slipped down over my eyes, and when I stood up and raised my glove to lift it, someone slashed my skates out from under me and I fell again. I heard more laughter and people were slapping the glass above me. The play had moved down ice by the time I got up, and I had to chase it.

The hits came regular after that. Every player on the Clippers slammed into me whenever they could. I was slashed repeatedly from behind. I was cross-checked, tripped, held and elbowed. When someone pushed my face into the glass with his forearm, I spun on my skates. My helmet fell off, and I was standing toe to toe with the tall centre. He flipped his gloves off, spread his skates wide, raised his fists and scowled at me.

"Whatta ya gonna do, squaw hopper?" he asked.

I looked over at our bench. Virgil was standing there looking at me. As I bent to retrieve my helmet, the boos rained down from the stands. There was clutter strewn all over the ice. The crowd was rabid. Back on the bench I slumped down and took a long swig from the water bottle. I could feel my teammates all looking at me. I stared at my feet.

"You don't gotta take the cheap stuff, Saul," Eagle Chief said. "Hit the fuckers back."

"That's not my game," I said.

"Starting to look like it better be."

When I went out for my next shift, the crowd was on me right away.

"Hey, it's Chief Chicken!"

"Injuns are s'posed to wear war paint, not make-up!"

"Hit 'em with your purse, Indian Horse!"

As I leaned in for the faceoff, their centre blew me a kiss. "Pussy," he sneered. He slashed the stick out of my hands when the puck was dropped. When I skated away he raised his hands to the crowd and they roared.

They kept at me all through the game, and when it was over I was covered in welts and bruises. And we lost. That hurt far more. I sat in the dressing room holding ice to the most painful areas.

"Tough guys," Virgil said.

"We could have won," I said.

"Hard when they won't let you skate."

"Where the hell were the refs?"

"You sound like a whiner."

"Hey, you saw how they played me."

"Yeah. I saw. I saw how you reacted, too."

"You think I'm chicken?"

"I think you're scared, yeah. I would be if I was your size. There's some big boys in this tournament. It ain't gonna get any easier now that they know how to slow you down."

Virgil was right. It didn't get any easier. It got worse. Every team we faced after that sent their biggest and toughest out against me. They sent their finesse players out against our other lines, so that when my teammates tried to hand out a measure of punishment they were penalized and played short-handed a lot of the time. The Moose struggled. My body was sore. My thighs had been slashed so many times I could feel the beginnings of a charley horse. When we came out for our last game, a game we had to win to stay in the tournament, I didn't know if I had it in me. For the very first time that I could remember, I couldn't find the vision. I couldn't seem to read the play and I felt hopeless. I felt like a loser. On my first shift in

that game I was skated hard into the boards by both opposing defensemen and had my head rubbed into the glass for
extra measure. When I turned, the biggest of them pushed
me in the chest and I fell back into the boards. He waited,
as I gathered myself, settled my helmet square on my head
and skated away. He spat at my feet as the crowd booed
lustily.

When I finished that shift I came back to our bench and
tilted my head up to squirt water from the bottle onto my
face. That's when I felt it. Spittle. It rained down from the
seats behind us, and I heard them calling me names and
beating against the glass. When I turned around I came
face to face with a boy who must have been about nine. He
spit against the glass. "Fuckin' chicken," he mouthed. The
man standing beside him squeezed his shoulder.

By now, the whole crowd was on its feet and gesturing
toward our bench. When the ref had whistled the game
down, he skated to the PA announcer. It took a full five
minutes for the crowd to settle down. While they cleaned
the garbage off the ice we went to our dressing room. I sat
with my head down, and no one said a word. When I looked
around, nobody would meet my eye.

There are times in this world when you have to look
hard at yourself. The challenge you feel is the one that
burns in your gut. I knew my team wanted me to buckle.
They wanted me to bare my fists and fight. But I would
not do that. I would not surrender my vision of the game. I
would not let go of my dream of it, the freedom, the release
it gave me, the joy the game gave me. It wasn't anybody
else's game to take away from me. Father Leboutilier had

said that it was God's game. I had no head for that idea. But I knew for a fact that the game was my life. I sat there in that horrible silence and I smouldered. I raged, and when the referee knocked on the door I stood up with the others to head back to the ice. I clomped with them down the hallway, and when I got to the bench I turned and looked at the crowd. I raised my stick to them and stepped out onto the ice and reclaimed the game.

There wasn't one of those players who could skate with me.

33 ———

Two things came out of that tournament. The first thing was that it made me tougher. I would not fight, but I was better able to handle the rough stuff after that; to churn my legs and use my weight to flail through and make the pass that cleared the logjams they set up for me. I ignored the slashes, spears and elbows. I never saw the sense in fights. They always sent their goons to goad me. But I never fought.

The second thing was the press clippings. It had been a colossal struggle, but we'd fought back to win that big tournament. When we hit the road back to Manitouwadge, every one of us was spent. Wasted. But we'd won it. There was something in the negativity from the crowds and the other teams that drove us. My teammates had wanted me to drop my gloves and start throwing punches, but they'd all felt the splatter of the spit that rained down, and every player on the Moose took that personally. We pushed ourselves to excel, to show them that the game belonged to us too. So we were champions, and they wrote about us in all the newspapers. Virgil saved the clippings in a plastic folder.

Soon after those stories appeared, we started to see a stranger in the stands. He was a tall, thin white guy in a battered hat and a long grey trench coat. Wearing those pullover rubbers with the zippers you never see in the North. He showed up at a tourney in Osnaburgh, and then at one in Pickle Lake. He was in the stands during the big tournament in Batchewana, and as we clomped back into our dressing room after winning the semifinal, the word "scout" was whispered along the line. I sat down on the bench with a towel draped around my neck and everybody looking at me. Big brown faces. Deep dark eyes. Indian faces, all stoic and quiet, studying me with a focus that rattled me some.

"What?" I asked.

"He's here for you, Saul," Ernie Jack said quietly.

"Who is?"

"The scout."

"Nobody knows if he's a scout or not."

There was a knock at the door, and Virgil walked over and opened it. The white guy stood there with his hands thrust deep in the pockets of his coat. He and Virgil talked in low voices for a moment or two. There wasn't a sound in that room. No one moved to undress. I could see the man scanning the room, and when his eyes fell on me he squinted. Then he patted Virgil on the shoulder and Virgil closed the door. He crossed the room and sat down beside me. You could have heard a pin drop in that room.

"Guy's name is Jack Lanahan. He's a scout for the Leafs," Virgil said. "Says he'd like to talk to you."

"About what?"

Virgil laughed and slapped my knee pad. "What the hell does a big scout like that talk about, Saul? He thinks you could play in the NHL."

"I've never been out of the North."

"Well, maybe this is your ticket out."

"Never thought about going anywhere."

"That's because you never been scouted before. Talk to him."

—— 34

I found Lanahan sitting in the stands reading a sports magazine. His raised eyebrows pushed down on his nose and the little glasses made him look like he was surprised at what he was reading. He folded the magazine when I approached and stuffed it into his pocket. He stood up and shook my hand.

"Jack Lanahan, Saul. Nice to meet you."

"Same."

"Your captain told you what I'm doing here?"

"Some."

"What do you think about that?"

"Not much."

He laughed and sat down and motioned for me to join him. I sat a few seats away. "That rush in the third period? You had the puck for forty-eight seconds. You went end to end with it, dipsy-doodled around awhile, then made that pass behind your back to your left defenseman scooting in from the blue line. How'd you know he was coming?"

Lanahan took off his glasses and folded the arms carefully and slipped them into the inside pocket of his coat. He crossed one leg over the other and folded his hands in his lap. When he caught me studying him he just grinned and threw an arm across the back of the seat beside him. Patient. Calm. Didn't rattle.

"It's where he was supposed to go," I said.

"What if he hadn't?"

I looked at him and shrugged. "He did," I said.

Lanahan laughed again, and I could hear the echo in the empty arena. "Yes, he did. But why wait to pass? You could have made a shot."

"It's a team game," I said.

"Didn't look like that for the first forty-eight seconds."

"Time stops when the puck is in the net."

He kicked the back of the seat in front of him. "It does, doesn't it? Saul, I think you could play at a higher level. I think with the right coaching and the right environment you could play pro. You're incredibly fast. You have a puck sense I've never seen before and you can take a hit despite your size. What would you say to that?"

"To what part?"

"The pro part."

"I never thought about it."

"Well, think about it now, because I could get you a try-out with the Toronto Marlboros. They're Major Junior A. The feeder club for the Maple Leafs."

"We've tried higher levels. It sucks."

"The Marlies aren't Espanola, Saul."

He looked at me evenly. He'd obviously done his research and I looked past him to the ice. He waited me out. I leaned forward in my seat. "White ice, white players," I said. "You gonna tell me that isn't the case everywhere? That they don't think it's their game wherever a guy goes?"

He took his time answering. "It's not a perfect country," he said. "But it is a perfect game."

"Is it?"

"Yes. That's why you play."

"How do you know that?"

"I've been scouting for a long time, Saul. I could never play the game. I didn't have the body for it. Bad eyes, bad genes, no stick, no shot. But I love it. God. So I head out on the road every winter and I go to hundreds of games in hundreds of dead-end little towns. The towns and the players are all different. But the game is always the same, its speed and power. Hockey's grace and poetry make men beautiful. The thrill of it lifts people out of their seats. Dreams unfold right before your eyes, conjured by a stick and a puck on a hundred and eighty feet of ice. The players? The good ones? The great ones? They're the ones who can harness that lightning. They're the conjurers. They become one with the game and it lifts them up and out of their lives too. That's what happens to you, isn't it?"

I looked right into his eyes and he held the look. "Yes," I said, finally. "It was like that right from the start."

"And I can see that when you take the ice. I don't think you see it like other players do, Saul. I think you see it from a different kind of plane. It takes a while for you to get to that. I've seen you sit back and watch, read the energy. You read the game and once you've got it, you jump in. Those blind passes? They aren't so blind, are they?"

"No," I said.

"You know how to make the ice work for you, Saul. That's why you should be playing at a higher level. You're wasted here."

"I've never been anything other than a Moose."

He turned in his seat to face me. "I know. But they've taken you as far as they can."

"I can't just leave."

"Sure you can. And they would want you to."

"How do you know that?

"Because they love the game too."

——— 35

It took them three weeks to get to me. We went to the scheduled tournaments and we played well, but there was a new energy on the team, not just on the ice but on the bench and in the dressing room. Waiting. Expectant. I didn't know what people wanted me to say, so I just played as usual. We were on our new team bus heading back from Pic River when four of them came to me. Virgil. Ernie Jack. Louis Greene. Little Chief. They huddled around my seat while I kept my face to the window.

"You gotta go, Saul," Virgil said.

"Don't want to," I said.

"That don't matter," Little Chief said.

"Why?"

"Because you got called."

"I don't follow." I stared out the window as the land peeled by, humped into spectral shapes by the moonless dark.

"We all play the game wishing that someday a call will come and someone will ask us to play with the big boys," Little Chief said. "Nobody says nothing about that. It must seem stupid on accounta we're just Moose, but we dream it anyhow."

"So that means what to me?" I asked.

Ernie Jack leaned over so I could look at him. He was big, wide in the upper body, so he ate up a big chunk of the darkness. He punched me on the thigh. "It means you get out," he said. "I'm twenty-three years old. I'm working graveyard in the fucking mine and I been there since I was sixteen. I'll be there until it kills me or I'm too fucking old. I ain't got no out. I don't mind that. I got Emma and I got the kids and I got the Moose until I'm too damn old for that too. But someone reached down and put lightning bolts in your legs, Saul. Someone put thunder in your wrist shot and eyes in the back of your fucking head. You were made for this game. So you gotta give this a shot for all of us who're never gonna get out of Manitouwadge."

"What if I don't make it?"

"You will," Ernie said.

"You believe that?"

"I ain't the one that has to believe it."

I turned to look at the triangulated shadow of the trees thrown up into the sky. I just wanted to play the game. I didn't want to have to make a choice.

"Something big's gonna happen to you if you stay here, Saul." It was Little Chief. I turned to look at him and all I could see was the outline of this head like a keg.

"What's that?" I asked.

"Well, I'm gonna wake up ten, fifteen, years from now and I'm gonna clump on down to the rink to skate and I'm gonna see you making circles on the ice with the puck. I'm gonna see you like I always seen you. Like something fucking special. And I'm gonna walk over to those boards, fifteen years down the road, all stiff and sore from lugging lumber around all day and see you there and know that it all could have been different. That I mighta been able to live some of my dream out through you. But you're still here. So the big thing that's gonna happen to you? I'm gonna pull you over those boards and kick the shit right outta you for wasting it. For not answering the call."

He thumped the back of the seat, and I could feel the emotion working in him. I looked at Virgil. "What do you think?"

"I think you owe me."

"I owe you?"

"Yeah."

"Owe you what?"

"You owe me the game."

"How's that?"

"I was the one who said okay, you skate with us. My dad got you out of that school and brought you up here. But it was me who said yes for the team. I coulda said you should play bantam or midget first. But I saw what you could do and I knew that you could make this team better. If you weren't a Moose you'd be nowhere. No one woulda seen you, hearda you, known about you. There wouldn't be a scout knocking on the dressing room door. So, yes, Saul, I gave you the game and you owe me."

"And if I don't go?"

"Then I'll think you're a coward. That you let it beat you without even trying."

"What if I'm not good enough?"

He laughed, and the others laughed too. "You're a shape-shifter, Saul. We all know that. The NHL never seen a shape-shifter before. Believe me, you'll be good enough."

"You sure of that?"

"Like he said, I ain't the one that has to be."

36 ———

In the end I played out the season and I agreed to go to the Marlboro training camp the next fall. I didn't want the pressure of landing there midway through their season. I didn't want to leave Manitouwadge just like that. I'd come to feel that the Moose, the Kellys and the town were mine. I went to school, I'd started working part-time at one of the mills, I was known wherever I went. I'd come to a place in the world that I could live in forever. Wanted to live in forever. I couldn't leave before I was ready.

Making myself ready was hard, but Virgil stayed by my side. We ran the hills outside of town. We did wind sprints up and down those rugged slopes and he pushed me harder than I had ever been pushed before. He cut an eight-foot length of birch, made me put it across my shoulders and run uphill with it. He made me bound the talus boulders, like Father Leboutilier and I had done, only now I did it with a thirty-pound pack on my back. He fashioned a harness out of a broom handle and some rope and I used it to raise fifty-pound bags of cement off the floor by rolling my wrists. We went to the dump, where he set up rows of tires and had me jump back and forth between them with my feet tied together. When I got so I could do that easily, he made me do it faster. I took a lot of tumbles among the trash. Occasionally, he took me to the bush and I'd chop a tree down. It would take hours, the axe in my hands getting heavier and heavier as I bulled my way through it. Afterwards, we'd buck the length of it with a saw and carry the branches and detritus to a slash pile for burning. Then he made me carry the sawn rounds to the truck, where he'd watch while I split them for firewood with a thirty-pound maul. It was immensely tough work, but I got stronger. I got leaner. I felt powerful

When the time came to leave, he walked me to the bus. I said goodbye to Fred and Martha and the boys on the Moose, but it was Virgil who took me to the Greyhound station. Manitouwadge was quiet. It was late August. I was almost seventeen. I was as tall as I would ever be, but Virgil had managed to pack muscle onto every inch of me. My forearms bulged like Popeye's and my thighs swelled against my pant legs. We didn't say much to each other as we walked through town. The sun sent shimmers of late summer heat up off the pavement. Flies buzzed around our faces. Pine gum and sulfur bit at our noses.

"I'm gonna miss this place," I said.

"Manitouwadge? Nothing to miss, really."

"I feel like I grew up here."

"Guess you did. You were a slack-bellied little pup when you got here." He punched me on the shoulder. "You worked damn hard, Saul. You'll do good down there."

"They've billeted me with a white family."

"Yeah. There's not many Indians down there probably. I've never been there. Toronto. But I can't imagine many skins really wanting to hang out in that big smoke and noise."

He stopped to light a cigarette. He offered it to me and I took a long drag before returning it, though I rarely smoked. We sat on the set of steps outside the bus station and watched traffic eke by. "You're like a brother to me. You know what I mean?"

"I had a brother once," I said.

"What happened to him?"

"I never talk about it."

He stubbed out his cigarette on the step. "My dad never talks about the school," he said. "Mom neither. And they don't say anything about what happened before that. Maybe someone just gave you a chance to rub the shit off the board once and for all."

He looked at me. "I don't know a whole lot about a whole lot of things. But if I know one thing for dead certain, Saul, it's that hockey is what you were sent here to do."

"What if I don't make it down there?"

"Then you don't make it, but at least you'll have been out there rattling the cage."

"Virgil? Thanks for everything."

"Don't sound so damn final. You can come back anytime."

"All right."

"All right."

He stood beside the bus as we rolled out, one hand above his eyes to block out the sun, the other raised in a kind of salute. When the driver swung the bus out onto the main street, Virgil disappeared. I sat in my seat and stared at the floor. I wanted to cry, but I didn't. Instead, I watched the land. Watched it stream by in lakes, rivers, trees and huge upward thrusts of rock until I fell asleep.

37

Toronto was a chimera, I thought as soon as I saw it. I'd learned about that monster in a book on mythology that I'd borrowed from the school library in Manitouwadge. The chimera was a fire-breathing beast with a lion's head, a goat's body and a serpent's tail. I liked mythology. The stories reminded me of the stories my grandmother would tell around the fires late at night. Reading them made me feel good. I read a lot while I was with the Kellys. Books had been my safe place all the time I'd been in the school and they still represented security, and whatever corner I huddled in to read was a safe one to me. But Toronto was like the chimera—a gross combination of mismatched parts. It was a mad jumble of speed, noise, and people. It dried up my eyes, and I could taste soot and oil and gas all the time. There were trees, but none of the big pines or spruce or fir I was used to. There were no rocks. There was nothing wild. The one time that I stepped out late in the evening and surprised a raccoon in the trash pile we stared at each other in amazement. Him to see an Indian in that jumble of glass and steel and concrete, me to see a creature meant for hinterlands where the wind carried animal sign instead of rot and decay.

I was billeted with an old couple called the Sheehans. The Irish were a tribe too, I supposed, because it was Lanahan who'd made the arrangement. The Sheehans were hockey people. Patrick had played until a knee injury ended things when he was thirty-nine, and Elissa, his high school sweetheart, had also grown up with the game. They were Leaf fans, and their home was decorated with the memorabilia of adoration. The room they put me in had a Toronto Maple Leafs pennant on the wall, and a huge Leafs bedspread and foot mat. The hallways were lined with pictures of every player they had billeted who made it to the NHL.

They were good to me. Elissa cooked magnificent suppers, and the refrigerator was open territory at any time of day. Patrick was a voluble raconteur about all things hockey. He regaled me with stories about George Armstrong, Jim Neilson, and an up-and-coming Indian kid named Reggie Leach, who people said would set the record books afire.

"So there's been a trail blazed for you, Saul. Native players aren't unfamiliar in the NHL."

We were just unfamiliar to the world *around* the NHL, I guess. When I showed up for rookie camp I was the only brown face in the room. Once the scrimmages began, none of the other players would call to me or send the puck my way. They weren't rough or violent. They just ignored me. I skated around the perimeter of the play like I didn't exist. But god, they were fast. They were all great skaters, and the precision with which they made plays was jaw-dropping. These were elite players culled from elite teams, so they were a joy to watch. I didn't mind much being shunted out of the flow. It gave me time to read them.

The second day of practice we were split into red and blue squads. I got a red jersey and lined up at the bench to be given my line assignment. I nodded to my new line-mates, though they didn't return my greeting. This was the first skate where players would be cut, and there was a high tension in the air. The Marlboros had room for three rook-ies that year, and there were thirty of us at camp. Forwards came through the neutral zone like rockets. Defensemen made passes like they were shots on goal, hard and accu-rate as rifle shots. Goalies were limber and quick as cats. I was stunned by what I saw. I was on the right wing when our line hit the ice, and I skated back and forth marvel-ling at the speed and dexterity of the players. When we got back to the bench, my centre elbowed me hard in the ribs.

"Skate," he hissed. "You make me look bad, I'll punch your lights out."

"All right," I said. I pushed my helmet down hard on my head.

On the next shift I kept my word. I was borne up on the crackle of energy around me, and when I cut into the play the first time I felt fleeter and more nimble than I ever had. These were some of the best players from across the coun-try. They made me work just to get clear. But the muscle Virgil had built onto me served me well. When the bigger players leaned on me I managed to push them off. When they tried to pin me along the boards, my legs were strong enough to skate out of the jam. The occasional slashes and cross-checks didn't even register. These players were so fast, so disciplined, so precise that it made me reach deeper, fight harder, skate more deliberately. Finally, on my fifth

shift, I took the puck from end to end. I circled the opposition net, spun in a loop-the-loop through the faceoff circle
and wristed a pass onto the stick of our left-winger, who
tapped it into the open net. I glided back to the bench and
slumped down beside our centre and elbowed him lightly
in the ribs.

"Skate?" I asked. "Like that, you mean?"

He stared straight ahead.

38

I made the team as a rookie, and I had a new weapon in my arsenal now. Trust. I trusted that these elite players would go to the right place, make the right moves, put themselves exactly where they needed to be. My passes were the solder that welded our attacks together. I loved the thrill of knowing that I'd sent someone into open ice, left them a gap in the defense, a lane that led to the mouth of the goal and that blinking red light. I scored when I could, but my passing game became electric. I made the Marlboros as a centre. A playmaker. A skater.

If hockey had been the only arena in which I was tested, I would have won in a rout. But it wasn't. I was still the Indian kid from northern Ontario. During a press interview following the announcement that I had made the team, I mentioned learning the game in broken-down boots with horse turds for hockey pucks. That made me even more of an oddity. No matter what I did, I remained the outsider. My teammates never called me Chief, but they didn't use my name either. They never called me anything but "thirteen."

"Thirteen don't talk much."

"I heard they're like that."

Or, "Thirteen never smiles."

"None of them do."

They took my passes, though. They let me fry that ice with my speed and hurtle forward with the puck. They allowed me to carry the game sometimes, waiting until I flipped the rubber to them. But they came out of a system that culled elite kids from the pack and made them special. They'd grown up with hockey moms and dads driving them to practice through sleepy morning streets, coaches they'd known for years pushing them to excel, fans expecting big results from their gifted kids. These guys weren't mean. They weren't vicious. They were just indifferent, and that hurt a whole lot more. I'd leave the shelter of the game and walk the streets of the city in something close to desolation. I lived only for the whistle that started the game.

Every team we faced that season was cut from the same cloth as the Marlies. The players were fast, precise, unrelenting and creative. They were warriors. They played at such a tempo that all I had to do was close my eyes on the bench and the vision settled over me right away. I was a whirlwind in those first games, and nobody could miss that. But the press would not let me be. When I hit someone, it wasn't just a bodycheck; I was counting coup. When I made a dash down the ice and brought the crowd to their feet, I was on a raid. If I inadvertently high-sticked someone during a tussle in the corner, I was taking scalps. When I did not react to getting a penalty, I was the stoic Indian. One reporter described how I looked flying across the opposition blue line with the puck on my stick: I was as bright-eyed as a painted warrior bearing down on a wagon train. This explosively fast, ordered game I was learning to play had set me on fire. I wanted to rise to new heights, be one of the glittering few. But they wouldn't let me be just a hockey player. I always had to be the Indian.

The fans picked up on it. During one game they broke into a ridiculous war chant whenever I stepped onto the ice. At another, the announcer played a sound clip from a cheap western over the PA. When I scored, the ice was littered with plastic Indian dolls, and once someone threw horse turds on the ice in front of our bench. A cartoon in one of the papers showed me in a hockey helmet festooned with eagle feathers, holding a war lance instead of a hockey stick. The caption read, "Welcome the new Marlboro man."

Soon, players on other teams were following suit. I was taunted endlessly. They called me Indian Whores, Horse Piss, Stolen Pony. Elbows and knees were constantly flying at me. I couldn't play a shift that didn't include some kind of cheap shot, threat or curse. And when I refused to retaliate, my teammates started leaving a space around me on the bench. I sat alone in that territory of emptiness, eight inches on either side of me announcing to everyone that I was different, that I was not welcome even among my own. Finally, it changed the game for me. If they wanted me to be a savage, that's what I would give them.

I began to skate with the deliberate intention of shoving my skill up the noses of those who belittled me, made me feel ashamed of my skin. One night against the London Knights I made a no-look backhand pass through the legs of one player over the outstretched stick of another, right onto the stick of our right-winger. He scored on a clear-cut breakaway. As we were skating back to our bench the Knights centre slashed me behind the knees and I fell to the ice. There was no whistle. The crowd howled. My teammates even laughed. He was seated on the Knights bench by then and I skated over lazily. They all looked at me and made faces. I flipped my right glove off at the last second and drove my fist right into this face. I fought three of them before they hauled me off the ice. That was the end of any semblance of joy in the game for me. I became a fighter. If an opposing player directed any kind of remark toward me, I dropped the gloves and started swinging. Any questionable hit was sufficient excuse for a tilt, and my bodychecks were hard, vicious and vindictive. I was bitter. I wanted the game to lift me up. To make the world disappear as it always had. But as a Marlboro, I could never shake being the Indian. So I became a puck hog. Instead of making passes to my open teammates, I skated and whirled until I could make the shot myself. One night, after an end-to-end rush that resulted in a goal on a nifty change of direction at the goal mouth, I dropped to one knee at the other team's blue line and mimed taking a shot at the net with a bow and arrow. It infuriated the crowd. The other team sent their biggest, toughest player after me on the next shift, and the fight that followed was titanic. I drew a game misconduct penalty and marched to the dressing room, bloodied but filled with a roaring pride.

"We didn't bring you here for this, Saul," the Marlies coach said to me in his office after the game. "We brought you here to be a player. Not some cheap goon."

"Hey, I'm just giving them what they want," I said.

"Who?"

"The crowd, the team. Don't you read the papers? I'm the Rampaging Redskin."

"That was an unfortunate bit of cheap writing. I'm sorry you had to go through that," he said.

"Yeah, well, maybe I'm better suited to a tomahawk than a hockey stick."

"You and I both know that's not true."

"I'm the Indian. That's all they see."

He started to bench me for long stretches in games. When I hit the ice I was effective. I scored twenty-three points in nine games. But the taunting from the stands continued, and I fumed and smoldered and racked up one hundred and twenty minutes in the penalty box. I caused the Marlies to play short-handed a lot of the time, and we lost seven of those games. Finally, they benched me completely. After one night of sitting in the stands, I packed my bag and got on a bus back to Manitouwadge.

39 ——

There was a girl I remember from St. Jerome's. Her name was Rebecca Wolf and she arrived there with her younger sister. They were beautiful. When I saw them for the first time they were getting out of the car that had brought them to the school. I was raking grass, but I stopped what I was doing to watch them. Rebecca saw me looking and gave me a little smile.

Rebecca's skin was clear and brown, and her eyes shone. She was tall for her age and slender, not gawky like other girls her age. I'd see her in chapel or walking through the hallways. I'd try to get her to notice me, but she almost never did.

Rebecca's sister, Katherine, was small and timid. She was scared of the nuns, but when she tried to run to her older sister for comfort, they strapped her and locked her in a broom closet for hours at a time. Then they started putting her in the Iron Sister.

The last time they brought Katherine up from the basement, she was broken. She began to wet her bed at night, and the nuns beat her for that. They would haul her into the aisle and strap her. When Rebecca tried to protect her sister she earned a trip to the basement herself. And while she was down there, Katherine died. No one knew what happened. She went to bed and the other girls found her dead in the morning.

They didn't bring Rebecca up from the Iron Sister for four days. When they told her she just looked at the faces of the nuns and didn't react. Then she turned slowly, walked to the front entrance of the school, and stood at the top of the stairs and screamed. She tore at her hair and face. No one moved to help her, for fear of retaliation from the nuns. But her wailing and sobbing cut all of us kids to the quick.

I was in the barn alone the next evening, practicing my shooting on the linoleum. I was so intent on the mechanics of my wrist shot that I missed the first few notes. But those that followed made me raise my head and listen. A voice shimmered through the evening air, and I walked to the door of the barn to see where it came from. Rebecca was standing in the rough grass of the Indian yard, her palms raised to the sky, and she was singing in Ojibway. It was a mourning song. I could tell that from the feel of the syllables. Her agony was so pure, I felt my heart ripped out of me. I stood crying in that doorway, offering what prayers I could for the spirit of her sister.

I never saw the knife. Not until the song was over. She knelt on the fresh-turned earth of her sister's grave and slipped the knife from her coat and plunged the knife into her belly. As I ran to her, a whole crowd of kids burst from the school. She was dead when we got there, blood everywhere. We stood in a circle gazing down at her. No one said a word. No one could. But when someone began to sing the song Rebecca had sung we all joined in, the out-law Ojibway rising into the air. When the song was over, we filed back into the school, past the nuns and the priests who'd gathered at the bottom of the stairs. None of us looked at them.

————— 40

It was late at night when I got back to Manitouwadge. I walked from the bus to the Kelly house, knocked on the door and then waited on the steps with my bag at my feet. After a minute I heard footsteps. The door opened and closed, and Virgil sat down beside me in the dark. He lit a smoke. We sat there staring at the lights of the mill.

"What happened?" he asked.

"It was for shit," I said.

"Read about you. The Rampaging Redskin."

"That and more," I said. "Lots more."

He snapped the butt away with one finger, and we watched it spin through the night and land in a rut in the road. "You ripped it up, though, didn't you?" he asked finally. "Twenty two points in nine games."

"Twenty three," I said.

"Jesus, Saul. That's a season for most guys."

"So were the penalty minutes."

"You had to fight back. Shit, I know that. Glad you finally learned, actually."

"You got a spot for me on the Moose?"

"Hell, yeah. But what about the NHL? With stats like

that over a full season in Major Junior, you'd be a lock to be drafted."

"I just want to play the game, Virg. I can't do it with all that bullshit getting in the way."

He nodded. "So, what are you gonna do now?"

"Go to work, I guess."

"Mines or mill. That's all you got to pick from around here."

"I know. It's good enough for you."

"You were born for more, Saul."

"Says you."

We sat in the dark, and there were no more words. The silence was enough. Finally, he reached out to clap me on the back. After he went in I stayed out there a while looking up at the stars. When the chill got to be too much, I picked up my bag and walked into the house to sleep.

—— 41

Fred Kelly got me on a forestry crew as a deadfall bucker that fall, and I became a working man. When trees fell down or when the wind knocked them over I took a chainsaw and cut them into lengths that the log skidders could haul to the trucks. It was hard, heavy work, but there was something in the strain that I liked. I took to picking up eight-foot lengths of log and bearing them out of the tangle on my shoulders. I became known as a hard worker, industrious, and after a few weeks the company shipped me off to their logging camp on the shores of Nagagami Lake.

It took a float plane to get us in, and I watched the great green carpet of the land roll out below my face pressed to the window. When we landed I could feel it all around me, like the press of a living thing. The view from the bunkhouse was stark and beautiful. Any fear I'd carried about my first venture into the bush as a logger vanished. I'd stand on the rocks in the dim hours before any of the others had woken and feel it enter me like light. I'd close my eyes and feel it. The land was a presence. It had eyes, and I was being scrutinized. But I never felt out of place. Late in the evenings I'd walk into the trees, stride through the bush until I was wrapped in it, cocooned. The stars that pinwheeled above spun a thousand light years away. Time, mystery, departure and union were there all at once. I wondered if this was what it meant to be Indian, Ojibway. A ritual. A ceremony, ancient and simple and personal. If I could have borne it with me into the day-to-day life of the camp, things might have been different.

But they weren't. These were northern men, Finns, Swedes, Germans, Quebecois and Russians. They were lumberjacks. They were as efficient with the giant two-handed rip saws, axes and horse teams as they were with chainsaws and tractors. They were steeped in the tradition of it. They were huge, brawny men who bellowed and roared and skipped back and forth between languages over the course of a conversation, so I never knew where the gist of it was leading. Drinkers. Hard and deliberate. They spent their evenings in the loquacious flow of liquor, smoking and playing cards. Brawls erupted quickly and ended the same way. Then they'd return to their game, the blood of them cut with the next fresh deal, fists clutching cards like a throat.

They didn't know what to make of me. There hadn't been an Indian in their midst before. So I never joined them in their evening distractions. When I came back in from the bush I'd huddle in my bunk and read. When they started calling me "Chief" and "Tonto," "Geronimo" or "wagon burner," I'd heard it so often before that I didn't offer a reaction. That bothered them. I suppose they took my silence for high-mindedness, the books in my hands as a rebuff. They began to take my measure in the only way they knew how.

They'd push me hard in the woods and wait to see if I could keep up. I always could. When they pressed hard with their saws and axes through the trunks of great trees I did the same and I carried heavy lengths of sawn timber through the bush without a complaint. They tried to find a weakness in me, but I was determined that they would not. So they made it personal. They saw to it that I drew the assignment to clean the outhouses. I dumped lime and swept and batted at the flies that congregated in swarming masses. I washed dishes. I mopped the kitchen floor, carted garbage and shovelled up the mess bears and raccoons left scattered about the small gravel pit the camp used as a landfill. I oiled and greased tractors, hosed down trucks and skidders and washed down the bunkhouse each day before my shift started. The more they tried to exhaust me, the harder I worked. I did all of it without saying a word. Then I'd lie in my bunk and read by flashlight after they tumbled into bed and be awake and in motion by the time they rose.

They took to more insulting name-calling and swearing at me. Even when they took to pushing me and tripping me and swiping at me when I passed, I'd just level a blank look at the offender and keep on with the work.

Only on the land did I find calm. There I could relax. I could rest. I could sit looking out across the wide expanse of lake forever. But the time always came to turn back to the bunkhouse. I'd squint hard at the lighted windows of the camp and I'd draw into myself. I'd haul in a lungful of air, hold it, compact all my dark energy until it sat in my gut like a black marble, cold and glassy and hard. Then I'd walk back into their midst and they'd stop their game and challenge me. I'd walk to my bunk and lie down and read long into the night.

Then one night a big Swede named Jorgenson called to me, gestured crudely toward me. I stared at the ceiling for a moment. Then I rolled off the bunk and walked slowly to the table where he sat playing cards. As they laughed, I planted my feet wide. Jorgenson stood up and swung a meaty fist at my face. I blocked his punch with my forearm and reached out with my other hand and latched onto his throat. I squeezed. Hard. I walked forward slowly with the man's throat in my hand, wordlessly, lifting and pushing and squeezing at the same time. The big Swede clutched and grabbed and swatted at me, but the pressure of my grip was so great he weakened and dropped to his knees, red-faced and gasping with his eyes bugging out. As I let him drop to the floor I punched him in the head with everything I had, and he crumpled onto the floorboards. I turned to face the rest of them. I was frigid blackness inside, like water under a berg. I wanted another one to stand, wanted another one to swing at me, invite me to erupt. But they stayed seated, and nobody spoke as I walked slowly over to the table and picked up Jorgenson's discarded hand of cards. I studied the cards, then smirked and tossed the hand back on the table.

"Game over," I said. They never bothered me again.

———— 42

When I came out, I brought the intensity of the bush camp out with me. I was seventeen. I was still a boy. But this mistreatment made me hard. When I took to the ice with the Moose, the anger funnelled out of me, and my game became a whirling, slashing attack. It didn't matter who we played. I played as hard against the white town teams as I did against reserve teams. There was no lively banter on the bench. Instead, I glared at the ice until they opened the gate to release me. I still had grace, the flowing speed, but my eyes were feral beneath my helmet. I blazed up the ice with locomotive force, and when anybody hit me, I hit back. When they slashed me I slashed back harder, breaking my stick against shin pads and shoulder pads. When they dropped the gloves with me I punched and pummelled until I had to be torn off by my teammates. There was no joy in the game now, no vision. There was only me in hot pursuit of the next slam, bash and crunch. I poured out a blackness that constantly refuelled itself. The game was me alone with a roaring in my gut and in my ears. I heard nothing else. When the other members of the Moose stopped talking to me, I knew that I was beyond them, the tournament teams and the game, forever.

43 ———

I left Manitouwadge the year I turned eighteen. I'd saved
enough of my wages to buy an older-model pickup truck
that was outfitted with a steel box to carry the tools I'd
assembled. There was no plan. I was just leaving. I was a
working man. Work was everywhere. The highway led west
to the prairies, the mountains and the Pacific coast, and I
had never seen any of them. But it wasn't a yearning for
new geography that drove me—it was my tiredness of the
old. The bush had ceased to be a haven. A vacant feeling sat
where the beginnings of my history had once been. That
part of myself was a tale long dead, one that held nothing
for me. So I was heading out to create whatever history I
could with muscle and will and no constraints. I was leaving the bush and the North behind. I didn't think I needed
them anymore. The echoes of those I'd travelled with slid
into the trees I was leaving behind.

The Kellys took my departure with worry, though they
didn't try to stop me.

"It will be tough, Saul," Fred Kelly said. "A working life
is made easier by a home. People. Noise. Distraction. They
fill you when you're tired and depleted."

"Feels like I've had enough noise and people for a while," I said.

"That Toronto business was hard," he said. I'd never told anyone about the ordeal of the bush camp.

"Yeah."

"But you can let it go. You can stay here, work, get a life under your feet."

"I've had a life." It came out blunt, hard, and I could see that it hurt him.

"I know," he whispered.

Virgil was characteristically blunt. "Feels like you're fuckin' running."

"I'm not."

"What would you call it?"

"I'm just moving on. Time for a change."

He levelled a long look at me. "We're supposed to be teammates. Wingers. You. Me. Nobody wins alone, Saul."

"I'm used to alone."

"You're used to thinking you're alone. Big difference."

"I'm not disappearing," I said.

He shook his head sadly. "Seems to me you already did."

44 ——

I stood in the kitchen and looked out to where the boards of
the backyard rink sat in the pale spring sun. There wasn't
a way that I could think of to tell them how the rage felt
against my ribs, how it tasted at the back of my throat. I
had to leave before I collapsed under the weight of it.

I took one last walk through the house, trying to memorize the degrees of light in each room and the sound my
footsteps made on the floorboards, the feel of the jamb of
the front door against my palms. Then I walked out to my
truck and was gone by the time I started the engine.

Medicine Hat. Fort Chipewyan. Wabasca. Skookum-
chuck. Tagish Lake. I worked in all those places and more.
The resonance of those names haunting me with memories. I followed the rumours of work that tumbled from the
lips of the men I met and became migratory, a wandering
nomad with my eyes on distant hills. I covered long charcoal stretches of highway, the undulating yellow line like
a river bearing me somewhere beyond all recollection. Or
that's what I hoped. I would drive unthinkingly. Music was
my constant companion. I loved it for its ability to fill space,
to occupy the empty passenger side of the cab of the truck,
and the rooms I rented in two-bit motels in the mill towns,

mining towns and work camps where I landed. I learned about it with the help of books, and once I discovered Dvorak's cello concerto, I turned to it again and again through my travels to suspend the desperation clutching at my gut. Work and music sustained me for a long time. I could vanish into them and surface at my choosing. I preferred being alone to inquisitive company. I became a carpenter, roofer, miner, lumberjack, highway paver, railroad labourer, dishwasher, hide scraper, ranch hand, tree planter, demolition worker, steel foundry yardman and dock worker. I did not offer to be a buddy to my fellow workers. I did not become chatty. I did not move beyond the safety of the wordless barrier I erected between myself and other people. The rage was still there. It sat square in my chest whenever I heard "Chief," "Tonto," "Geronimo," "dumb Injun" or the hundred other labels men applied to me. But I never reacted. I wouldn't risk the explosion I knew would follow. The feel of Jorgenson's throat in my hands. The blackness inside me. Instead, I threw myself harder into the discipline of labour, losing myself in the grunt work I favoured.

A part of me missed the banter of the bench and the dressing room, though; the brash gutter talk and the teasing. So I began eating lunch and supper in beverage rooms and taverns where working men slung jibes back and forth, engaging in verbal arm wrestles that bristled with energy. I would sit and listen. Drink it all in and grin at the wit, the laconic retorts, the garrulous drunken voices rambling on about everything that concerned a man. I'm not sure when I began to drink myself. I only know that when I did the roaring in my belly calmed. In alcohol I found an antidote to exile. I moved out of the background to become a joker, a clown, a raconteur who spun stories about madcap travels and events. None of them had actually happened to me, but I had read enough to make these tales come to life, to be believable and engaging. Amid the slaps and pokes and guffaws that greeted them, I discovered that being someone you are not is often easier than living with the person you are. I became drunk with that. Addicted. My new escape sustained me for awhile. Whenever the stories and the invented histories started to unravel, I'd move on to a new crowd in a new tavern, a new place where the Indian in me was forgotten in the face of the ribald, hilarious fictions I spun. Finally, though, the drink had me snared. I spoke less and drank more, and I became the Indian again; drunken and drooling and reeling, a caricature everyone sought to avoid.

Now I had a different reason for needing to be away. So I drifted. When I could find work I was mostly a high-functioning drunk, keeping just enough in hand to get me through the day, and then sinking into the drink alone when the day was over. I'd pass out listening to music or with a book cradled in my lap. I'd wake up in the early hours, switch off the light, take another few swallows and fall back asleep. You can live for years like that. You experiment to find out how much you need to swallow to get you past a certain chunk of hours, how much you need to walk steadily, without your hands shaking. I was an alchemist, mixing solutions I packed in my lunch kit to assuage the strychnine feel of rot in my guts. It was a dim world. Things glimmered, never shone.

—— 45

I don't know what brought me back to northern Ontario in 1978. I don't remember deciding to head there. I don't recall thinking of it. I just wound up near Redditt where my brother had found my family before we set out for Gods Lake.

I arrived on a rainy day without much money in my pocket. After I'd settled at a small motel, I made the rounds of mills and lumberyards, the railroad and a few construction companies. I managed to get onto a crew breaking up rock at a quarry and put in a good couple of weeks. But after that there was no work to be found. I was tired of my life, really tired, and I lost my ability to hold things together. Before long I was too broke to get out of town and too wasted to care. I hung around the draft joints cadging drinks and hoping for a break. I was at a table in the corner of a workingman's bar, almost passed out, when someone shook my shoulder.

"You need to wake up there, fella."

I looked up and I expected to see the waiter or a cop, but the man was older, white, dressed in coveralls, a John Deere hat and work boots.

"Why?" I slurred at him.

"I don't drink with sleepers," he said.

"Why the hell would you want to drink with me?"

"Ojibways are the best storytellers I know. Got a story or two in you, I imagine. Don't ya?"

"Maybe. If you're buying."

"I'll buy. You just sit up and look proud."

"Sitting up I can manage."

"All of us got pride. You just need to remember you have it. Your people? A real proud people. Been my pleasure to know a lot of them."

"That why you sat here? Because you're proud of who I am?"

"Proud of your people. Seems like enough to start a conversation, anyway. Sift is my name. Ervin Sift," he said and stuck out a hand.

I shook his hand limply, though I managed to grab the draft beers the waiter dropped firmly enough. Sift let me be, and I was grateful for the lack of talk.

"Eat?" he said after another round of drinks.

"I could, yeah."

He ordered us steaks with mashed potatoes and beans. When the food arrived, he folded his hands right there in the bar and offered a prayer. Embarrassed, I cast a look around to see if anyone was watching.

He lifted his head, folded his napkin in his lap. "Soon's we're done this we'll head on home." All I could do was stare at him.

Over the next three days he nursed me through a killer hangover. I'd come to and he'd be at my bedside with a wet cloth to wipe my brow or a cup of soup he'd hold while I sipped it. He talked to me when I got scared, calmed me down. When I was over the worst, he helped me walk out to the porch for fresh air. All through it, he never asked a question.

Erv Sift was a farmer with a good-sized acreage where he managed a dozen head of cattle, a few sheep, chickens and an old burro left over from when he'd had horses. He ran a wood-cutting operation to augment his income. His last woodman had walked off unexpectedly, and he needed someone to take over. I drove his extra pickup truck around and cut firewood from deadfall, from slash piles the forestry guys had left behind, or from trees other landowners needed cleared from their property. Sometimes I winched dead trees out of the bush. I hauled everything to Erv's woodlot, made sure the piles were arranged according to the kind of wood and the amount of time they'd been seasoned. It was easy work. I knew my way around timber, and I got to work alone. I delivered firewood to homes all over the area. It didn't pay any screaming hell, but it was good, honest work, and I felt that I owed it to him. He gave me a room in the farmhouse. He was a widower. His wife had died a decade before, and he lived alone. They hadn't had any children.

Erv didn't drink much and he was a good hand at the stove. He never charged me for my meals. There was nowhere to spend my money, so soon I had a bank account for the first time in a long time. I fell into the routine we'd set up, and there was a degree of comfort in it. But there was a restlessness in me, something that wouldn't settle.

46 _____

We'd play cards late into the night listening to the radio, and if I didn't feel like talking he never pushed me to it. Instead, I always felt like he could see into me and understood that there were territories in me that I never travelled. He was content to see me recover and get my feet under me again.

"Saul," he said. "You ever pine for anything other than this? Ever have dreams of family, your own home, things like that?"

"No time for dreams," I said. "I had some once. They didn't pan out. I don't have them anymore."

He looked squarely at me and I held the look. Then he nodded and let it go. That was the first real conversation we ever had. For the most part he let me work and let me be. We were friends. There were always more silences between us than words but we understood each other's need for privacy. I knew he missed his wife. He wore it like clothes. He told me some of it. How they'd been together almost thirty years. How he'd drive his father's tractor twenty miles just to park on the hill overlooking her house on the chance that he might see her. How he met her at a country dance and she knew who he was. Had seen him on the hill. A far-away look would fall over him and he'd light his pipe and sit back in his chair and smoke and I knew to let him be.

Erv Sift was an angel. I have no doubt of that. He understood that I bore old wounds and didn't push me to disclose them. He only offered me security, friendship and the first home I'd had in a long time. But there were times when I would get up suddenly and feel the need to walk, to be away. It billowed in me like a cloud. He wouldn't say anything and neither would I. I would walk beyond the boundary of his fields and into the bush. Most times I would just wander. Sometimes I would find a tree or a rock and sit there and look out over the land and let the silence enter me. For a while the effect of the land was enough to keep me grounded. But there were always things swimming around in me that I could neither hold on to long enough to comprehend or learn to live with. It was like the change in the air that comes before a storm. You feel the energy build but there's nothing you can do to stop it. That's what it was like for me.

When those times came I couldn't talk. There was no language for it. I suppose when you can't understand something yourself it's impossible to let anybody else in even if you're motivated to. I wasn't. The bleakness and me were old companions by then, and the only thing I knew how to do about it was to drink.

At first it was only a few furtive sips while I worked. Then it became longer periods of walking out alone and coming back when I knew Erv was asleep. Then it became a morning gulp or two. And then the roof caved in.

I sat out on the tailgate of the truck with the saws and the axes around me. I'd stopped to pick up a crock in town before heading out to where I was cutting a good sized deadfall of fir trees. The sun was out. The day sparkled. But I felt dead inside. There was no reason for it. Everything was on the rails and it was looking as though I could stay with Erv for as long as I wanted. The work was good. I had money. I had a friend. In the end, that was what busted it. As I sat there drinking I thought about how much I actually owed Erv, how much I owed him the truth about me, of where I'd been, what I'd done, the whole shebang. There was a part of me that really wanted to do that. There was a part of me that desperately wanted to close the gap I felt between myself and people. But there was a bigger part that I could never understand. It was the part of me that sought separation. It was the part of me that simmered quietly with a rage I hadn't ever lost, and a part of me that knew if the top ever came off of that, then I would be truly alone. Finally. Forever. That was the part that always won.

So I drank. I finished off that crock and threw the tools and gear into the box and drove back to Erv's place. He was gone. He was out making arrangements for a few head of cattle from another farmer thirty miles away. I put the tools away. Then I walked into the house and gathered my belongings. I stood in the emptiness of another kitchen in another house in another life that only meant to offer me shelter. I couldn't take it. I couldn't run the risk of someone knowing me, because I couldn't take the risk of knowing myself. I understood that then, as fully as I ever understood anything. I didn't know why it was that way with me. I only knew it was. I only knew that I would run and that I would always continue running because I'd learned by then that it was far easier to leave if you never truly arrived in the first place. So I drained the one bottle of wine Erv had under the kitchen sink, and when the buzz had me hard I scribbled a note telling him where he could pick up the truck, and I drove away. Again. I was on a Greyhound bound for Winnipeg within an hour, with another bottle in my coat and the taste of another dried-up dream in my throat.

47 ———

It's funny how bartenders always tell you to drink up. When you're lost to it like I was, you always drink down. Down beyond accepted everyday things like a home, a job, a family, a neighbourhood. You drink down beyond thinking, beyond emotion. Beyond hope. You drink down because after all the roads you've travelled, that's the only direction you know by heart. You drink down to where you can't hear voices anymore, can't see faces, can't touch anything, can't feel. You drink down to the place that only diehard drunkards know; the world at the bottom of the well where you huddle in darkness, haunted forever by the knowledge of light. I was at the bottom of that well for a long time. Coming back up to daylight hurt like a son of a bitch.

The first thing you have to realize is that what you need to survive is killing you. That's the tough part. There's relief after a few big, hard swallows. Everything gets endurable. You can actually convince yourself that things are going to be okay even though you know in your gut that they're not likely to. So you fess up and try to stop. Stubborn bastards like I was at the end come to believe that we know enough about the weaning to be able to handle it ourselves. We cut down. We measure. We time our shots.

It never works. We're always just as drunk as we always were because the only way to really stop is to stop. That's how I wound up in the hospital. The seizures hit me and I collapsed on a sidewalk in Winnipeg. They had to strap me down because the withdrawal terrors got real bad. I saw things I can't even begin to describe and I was reduced to an incoherent babble and thrashing about. After five days of enough medication, I calmed down. I held down my first solid food after seven days. I sat up in my bed after eight.

The social workers told me about the New Dawn Centre. They said it was the best place for Native people to get help. It was on a hundred acres or so of land north of the city, and it was calm and restful. I resisted at first. But the doctors told me what a mess I'd made of my body and how another bout of drinking like I did would likely kill me, and for some strange reason I listened. I don't recall wanting to listen. I just did. When I got here, though, it was all about getting strong enough to leave. I was as addicted to leaving as I was to the booze. But the funny thing is that as my head got clearer, so did my recollections, and it spilled out pretty much on its own. Getting to the part about that long, dark downward spiral let me surface into the light for the first time in a very long time. I don't know if I was glad for it. Not at first. I felt as though I stood there blinking before I could move.

48 _____

There wasn't much to write about after that, though. As hard as I tried, I couldn't come up with anything else. I felt dissatisfied. I thought I'd discover something new, something powerful that would heal me. That's what Moses said the whole thing was supposed to lead to. When it didn't, I took to walking in the bush alone again. I felt as though nothing had changed. I felt as though the only thing I had done was quit drinking. Only the land offered me any kind of solace. So I walked every day for a while and explored the territory behind the New Dawn Centre.

A family of beavers had a lodge in the middle of a small pond a few miles into the woods. I'd sit in the cedars and watch them. They were delightful. That day they stayed active all through the afternoon, and when they finally disappeared into their lodge, it was early evening and my chances of making it back to the centre were not good. I walked up to a small table of rock I knew of. There was a lot of deadfall there, and I gathered enough for a good fire. If anyone came looking for me, they'd see it.

The night was alive with stars. I lay on my back on the moss and watched them. The longer I watched them, the more I could sense the earth turning in the heavens. It was late when I fell asleep.

I don't know if I was awake or dreaming when I heard a sound in the trees. There was a slip of a moon in the sky and a low fog hung just above the ground. The air was still. The fog amplified every rustle of movement in the trees, and far off I could hear the cautious steps of deer. But the sound that woke me did not belong to an animal. It was like a moan, a low humming. It died off, then came again a moment later. This time I scanned the line of trees, but there was nothing. Only the fog. Then a shape began to appear. At first it was just a blur, but as I stared the dim shape moved closer. It didn't walk. It floated. My guts cramped with fear. But I couldn't take my eyes off it. The moan came again. It sounded desolate. Human.

I began to see the shape of a person and behind it something huge and lumbering. I was prepared to bolt, but the voice, now easing into an Ojibway song, held me in place. As the strange duo drew near, the human shape moved one arm, and I could see that the big shape behind it was a horse.

The sheaths of fog parted, and I was looking at a man I knew was my great-grandfather. He was dressed in a traditional smock and pants with a porcupine quill headpiece. In one hand he held an eagle wing fan, and with the other he led the horse by a rope braided from cedar root. His song was low, and he walked in the measured step of it, coming to a halt mere yards from me. Shabogeesick was old. Terrifically old and thin. I could see the jut of his bones beneath the smock, and the spray of wrinkles running down his face. But his eyes were sharp and steady, and he regarded me curiously. He raised the eagle wing fan and shook it at me. As he passed it over his body, I saw my father, my mother. My brother. My uncle. My aunt. My grandmother. I wept at the sight of them. My grandmother held a finger to her lips and crinkled the corners of her eyes at me. Then they turned, and the old man lifted my grandmother up onto the horse's back. My family walked slowly into the depths of the fog, and I could hear them singing as they retreated. I closed my eyes, feeling an incredible weight of grief and longing, and when I opened them again the slender silver arc of the moon hung high above me. The fire had died down. I threw another piece of wood on it and sat with my arms hugging my knees. I cried again as I stared into those orange flames. I sat there all night, and when the first grey light of morning eased upward I kicked dirt over the fire to kill it. I was leaving again. Only this time I knew exactly where I was going.

—— 49 ·

"**I don't know** why I have to go. I just know I do." That's what I told Moses.

He only studied me some and then nodded. He'd been around a long time and he knew drunks. "We're here if you need us," he said. "Don't forget that."

"I won't," I said.

Once I'd checked out, I caught the bus east and promptly fell asleep before we'd hit the highway outside of town. It was a dreamless sleep. I woke to a dull morning in the fog of northern Ontario, and while the bus refuelled I sat in a diner and drank coffee and had a small breakfast of dry toast and fruit. Everyone seemed as bleary as I felt. They took tables alone or meandered through the parking lot sipping coffee and smoking to kill the time. When we loaded up again I stared at the land flashing by. I remembered how I'd watched it as a kid in the back of that sedan with Lonnie Goose and the girl whose name I'd never learned.

White River hadn't changed all that much. It still looked like a northern mill town. There were newer chain stores now, and the main street had been widened. The old arena had been replaced with a newer, bigger version. The gravel road that had led out of town beyond the quarry was paved now. But the sweep of the land was still the same. Past the quarry it dipped down into lowlands, the marsh and the stream where we'd bagged suckers, then wound upward through thick bush. As the cab I'd caught rounded the last turn, I could see the school.

I paid the cab driver and stepped out at the head of the driveway. The old sign drooped sadly off one post. Someone had shot out most of the letters with a shotgun so that only the first *S* of *St. Jerome's* was legible. The post it hung on was nicked and bitten off by bullets. Old wine bottles and rusted-out beer cans were strewn about the ditch. Lumps of human excrement sat by the post itself. I unhooked the chain across the entrance and laid it on the ground. The cab driver honked as he pulled away. The driveway was pocked with potholes. The fields where they'd grown potatoes and cabbage and turnips were overgrown with weeds.

The school itself was crumbling. Hollow. All of the windows were smashed. The ones on the top floors had been shot out, bullet holes splayed on the sills and sashes. I could hear the flutter of birds from within and the coo of pigeons in the eaves. Graffiti covered the walls with epithets and damnations. The leak of them like blood. The scrunch of my steps echoed through the gaping windows. It was like being followed by ghosts.

The classrooms had occupied the first floor, and beneath their windows people had laid flowers. They were withered now, in bouquets wrapped in plastic and tied with string or ribbon. Here and there I saw a doll or a teddy bear. I knelt and picked up a small yellow truck and spun its wheels with my thumb. Inside, the desks had been smashed and the chalkboards torn from the walls. There was a heap of black rubble in the centre where someone had lit a fire that didn't take. The feel of the room on my face. Desolate.

The outbuildings were in ruins. I walked past them toward the barns. They too had been ransacked and they smelled of decay. The wet rot of hay and straw. When I rounded the back end, I saw that the boards of the rink were still standing, mostly, though the chicken wire that had stretched across the ends had rusted through. Coils of it hung down like webbing. I stepped through a break and stood in the mud and weeds. A pad of earth. That's all the rink was now. I knelt to touch it.

"You can't be here, mister."

An older, bent-legged man strolled toward me from around the corner of the barn. He was scowling, but the ruddy good health at his cheeks gave away the effort it took to create the look.

"I used to live here," I said.

"Don't matter. Lots of them used to live here, and you can see how heartwarming an experience the visits have been."

"I haven't seen it since the sixties."

"They closed her in '69. Fact is, she was pretty close to being done a few years before that. Most of the kids had run off, and no one could be bothered chasing them down anymore. The town's looking to sell the land."

"Ransacked pretty good?"

"There's nothing left now but junk. People still come here though. Some nights I see their fires. I generally wait until morning to chase them off. They're hung-over or just wore out by then. Sometimes it's the same ones. Time after time."

He stretched out a gaunt hand and I took it. "I'm Jim Gibney."

"Saul. Indian Horse."

"Jesus. That's a handle isn't it? Our Indians around these parts are mostly Foxes, Martins, Wasacases or Wabooses. How long were you here?"

"I left when I was thirteen. Came when I was a little guy."

Gibney swept an arm toward the rink. "You play when you were here?"

"Some."

"Any good?"

The rink was smaller than arena-sized ones. I saw that now. Its corners were sharper, and it was shorter by about fifteen feet. The boards weren't as high as they should have been, and I remembered us hunting pucks down in the thigh-high snow, heaving them back over the boards to the players, who waited impatiently, their breath like storm clouds in the crisp winter air. "They couldn't keep me on the team," I said.

"Well, not everyone's Gretzky. Listen, Saul, you take your time, and when you're ready to leave make sure you hook the chain back up at the head of the drive. Keeps the cows out, leastways."

"I'll do that."

As Gibney sauntered off, I walked over to the boards and propped my elbows on the top. The wood wobbled. The only sound was birds calling in the trees at the edge of the field. I closed my eyes, and in the still air I could hear the wild calls of boys and the sound of sticks clacking on ice and hard rubber pounding into board. I remembered the prick of ice crystals and the numb feeling in the soles of my feet in their thin rubber boots and the shovel in my hand as I worked, thrilled at seeing open ice emerge, each laboured breath making child's play of man's work.

I cried then. I stood there and looked at that sad ruin of a rink and wept. And suddenly, I remembered.

I remembered standing at the boards with Father Lebou-tilier on a perfect winter's day. The clouds of my breath rose around my face and the sound of the boys skating was magnified by the cold, still air. As we watched the scrim-mage, he pointed things out with his stick. I paid close attention. He pounded the top of the boards with one hand at a very nice play, and I did too. He turned to look at me and smiled. Then he rubbed my head with his hockey glove.

"This game brings out the best in you, Saul," he said.

I remembered the two of us alone in his quarters, watching a game on television. When the Canadiens scored a goal, we celebrated. I jumped up and down in boyish glee, and he clapped his hands. Then he stood up and pulled me toward him. He pressed my face into his body as he rocked back and forth on the balls of his feet. I could feel the broad warmth of his hand on the back of my head, smell his soap, feel the scratch of fabric on my skin and the buckle of his belt against my chin.

"My angel," I heard him say.

When he knelt down and cradled me in his arms, I felt no shame or fear. I only felt love. I wanted so much to be held and stroked. As he gathered my face in his hands and kissed me, I closed my eyes. I thought of my grand-mother. The warmth of her arms holding me. I missed that so much.

"You are a glory, Saul." That's what he always told me. It's what he whispered to me in the dim light of his quarters, what he said to me those nights he snuck into the dormitory and put his head beneath the covers. The words he used in the back of the barn when he slipped my trousers down. That was the phrase that began the groping, the tugging, the pulling and the sucking, and those were always the last words he said to me as he left, arranging his priestly clothes. "You are a glory, Saul." Those were the words he used instead of love, and he'd given me the job of cleaning the ice to buy my silence, to guard his secret. He'd told me I could play when I was big enough. I loved the idea so much that I kept quiet. I loved the idea of being loved so much that I did what he asked. When I found myself liking it, I felt dirty, repulsive, sick. The secret morning practices that moved me closer to the game also moved me further away from the horror. I used the game to shelter me from seeing the truth, from having to face it every day. Later, after I was gone, the game kept me from remembering. As long as I could escape into it, I could fly away. Fly away and never have to land on the scorched earth of my boyhood.

I felt revulsion rise in me. My throat was parched. Rage was a wild heat that rose out of the base of my spine and through my belly, and I punched those rotting boards until my knuckles were raw, the tears erupting out of me. I fell to the ground and buried my head in my arms. I had run to the game. Run to it and embraced it, done anything that would allow me to get to that avenue of escape. That's why I played with abandon. To abandon myself. When the racism of the crowds and players made me change, I became enraged because they were taking away the only protection I had. When that happened, I knew that the game could not offer me protection any longer. The truth of the abuse and the rape of my innocence were closer to the surface, and I used anger and rage and physical violence to block myself off from it.

When I sat up again, the sun was sinking low. A gathering chill rode in on the breeze that kicked up dust at my feet. It was a very long walk back to town, and I knew where I had to go from there.

50 ⸺

I slept on the bus ride north to Kenora. I stopped just long enough to eat in a small café, and then flagged a passing taxi that took me as far as Minaki. It was early afternoon when I got there. The town was still an underused railroad stop and work camp for railroad labourers. There were a lot of Ojibway people around, and from what I could see most of them were living in the rat-trap government houses in a hollow behind the upscale Minaki Lodge, which catered to moneyed tourists. I found someone in need of some fast cash with a boat and outboard motor, and I arranged to rent them. I loaded the boat with supplies, extra gas and a small tent. No one asked any questions. The boat owner was content with the handful of bills I gave him, and I saw him in the lineup for liquor while I was shopping. The sun was just starting to slip behind the trees as I aimed the boat downriver, in the direction of Gods Lake.

The river was like I remembered it, black as tea, swirling with secrets. The water level was high and the current powerful, turning the river into a huge, serpentine creature, undulating and curving. I mostly let the motor idle and allowed the river to haul me forward, giving it gas intermittently to stay in the deepest part of the current and avoid the huge rocks that sprang up irregularly in the hidden shoals.

The river opened wide into channels and gaps between spare rock islands and larger wooded clumps of land. The light eased down, giving the river's edge a mystical feel, and I remembered the stories my grandmother had told about how this waterway fed the souls of our people. The silence was profound. There was no wind. I eased the throttle back and kept one hand on the arm of the motor. I was like a piece of flotsam, borne wherever the current might take me.

As I felt the air chill, I headed for a larger island to make camp for the night. Before long I had a fire blazing. I sat close to it, warming myself as I stared into the flames. The land felt good around me, but there was a hollow ache in my belly now. Thought of the school filled my head and I could feel a moan building in my gut. As it escaped me, it frightened me with its ancient sound. I wrapped a blanket around myself, and curled into a ball and pressed my eyes tight.

You're free. That's what Father Leboutilier had told me that last time I saw him. Free to go where the game could take me. I shook with anger as I recalled it. I was never free. He was my captor, the warder of my innocence. He had used me. I felt hate, acrid and hot. "You are a glory, Saul." I repeated those words over and over, until the pressure inside forced me to my feet. I kicked at roots and stones and the jut of logs as I howled, ragged, rough and sore. When I couldn't scream any longer, I picked up the small hatchet I'd bought and began to whack at a stump. I hit it with everything I had, until my arms and shoulders burned and it seemed that every ounce of fluid in me had drained out through my sweat and tears. I hobbled to the river, waded in up to my knees and splashed water over me. I cupped my hands and drank. When I'd calmed some I walked back to the fireside, spent. I woke at dawn to smoke spiralling lazily from the dying fire and fog settled over the river. I broke camp and aimed the boat downriver.

51

I made Gods Lake by early afternoon. My insides still felt like sandpaper. There was an eerie silence as I made the portage, feeling the bush close off behind me. The shadows were deep and ominous. When I stepped out onto the western edge of the lake and looked across it, it was as though I had never left.

I'd never walked the shore of the lake completely. But I did so that day, and every step closer to our old family campsite transported me further back. The angst in my belly disappeared. My thoughts cleared. I walked in a peace I could not recall having experienced before. I reached out to touch the broad span of ferns, the trunks of trees, leaves, grasses. A part of me remembered each sensation. The smell in the air was rich and earthy, with a wisp of swamp and bog. Dying things and living things together. The air was filled with birdsong. I broke through the trees fifty yards from the foot of the cliff. As I knelt on the stone beach, gazing up at the cliff, the clouds at its upper edge moved as though it was a living being, breathing. I closed my eyes, close to weeping, and I heard my name whispered. I opened my eyes to see a flotilla of canoes gliding toward the shore.

Benjamin. My grandmother, with my Grandfather Solomon. My mother and father. Strangers I took to be ancient members of my family. Wind-tanned, leathery faces, deeply creased and lined. My people. And there was Shabogeesick himself, paddling solo in a birch bark canoe that looked ancient and brittle but rode the water like a wisp. He raised the flat of his paddle in salute, then beached his canoe and stepped ashore. He stood a pace away from me, studying me intently.

"You have come far," he said finally.

"Yes," I replied.

"The journey you make is good."

"What am I to learn here?"

He swept his arm to take in the lake, the shore and the cliff behind us. "You've come to learn to carry this place within you. This place of beginnings and endings."

I looked up to see an eagle circling the rim of the cliff. Shabogeesick laid a hand on my shoulder, and we were suddenly on the top of the cliff. He put a hide pouch in my right hand and a broad eagle feather fan in my left. Shabogeesick gazed at me kindly. I closed my eyes again, and when I opened them he was gone.

I stood on the edge of the cliff with my pouch and eagle feather fan and my family stood around the fire in the trees looking up at me. Soft singing, low like a prayer, came from the boats below. I took a pinch of the tobacco from the pouch and held it up to the evening star. As I did, the sky eased into purples and blues and indigos. The singing from below rose higher and the great northern lights emerged to dance beneath the unblinking eye of the moon. I cried in great heaving gasps. I let myself mourn. Allowed every ounce of sorrow and desperation, loneliness and regret to eke out of me. I cried until I couldn't cry anymore. Then I heard my name.

"Saul."

The moon hung in the sky like the face of a drum. As I watched, it became the shining face of a rink, where Indian boys in cast-off skates laughed in the thrill of the game, the smallest among them zooming in and out on outsized skates. I offered tobacco to the lake where everything started and everything ended, to the cliff that had made this the place of my people, and I offered my thanks aloud in an Ojibway prayer.

52 ———

I went back to the New Dawn Centre. I hadn't planned
on it. I hadn't planned on anything. The only thing I had
known for certain was that I had to backtrack, to revisit
vital places from my early life, if I was ever going to understand how to live in the present. Call it intuition, I suppose.
But I needed to go to the school just as I needed to return
to Gods Lake. So I went back to talk. I went back to learn
to share the truth I had discovered locked deep inside me.
I went back because I wanted to learn how to live with it
without drinking. I went back because I needed a solid start
on a new road and I knew it would be hard. Sometimes
ghosts linger. They hover in the furthest corners, and when
you least expect it they lurch out, bearing everything they
brought to you when they were alive. I didn't want to be
haunted. I'd lived that way for far too long as it was. So I
put in the winter there. I worked closely with Moses and I
learned how to lift the lid off my life and inspect what was
contained. It was hard work. It terrified me a lot of times,
but I made the journey, and when I felt strong, confident,
secure with my feelings and my new set of skills, I returned
to knock on a door that I hadn't knocked on in a long, long
time. It was just after the first thaw.

When Fred Kelly opened it, his face cracked into a wide grin. He'd aged well. His hair was silver and he'd gained a bit of weight. "Look who's here," he said. He held the door open and I walked in.

The house looked the same as when I'd left it. It was orderly and neat, with light pouring in through the windows, and filled with the smell of baking. I wondered how people could live with things set in place, fixed, their places determined by the power of the recollection they contained, the memories they held. It was what made a home, I believed; the things we keep, the sum of us. Fred excused himself and went upstairs, and I found a seat on the living room couch. When he came back, Martha was with him. They stood in the doorway with their arms around each other, looking at me without speaking. I stood up. None of us knew what to say.

"We should sit down," Martha said finally.

They took chairs opposite the couch. I sat on the very edge of it, my forearms on my knees and my hands clasped together. I tapped my toes nervously on the carpet. Martha stared at me, her eyes shiny with tears, balling the corner of her apron up in her fist. Fred reached over and put a hand over hers.

"Thought I'd know what to say once I got here," I said. "Turns out I don't."

Fred shrugged. "People put way too much stock in words. Sometimes it's better to just sit. Kinda get used to each other again."

"I never put stock enough in talk, really. But I'm learning how these days. More than I did before, at least," I said. "There are things I found out that I never told anyone."

"About the school," Fred said quietly.

"Yes."

"We know, Saul. We always knew," Martha said quietly. "Not specifically. But we were there too."

"They taught us to hide from ourselves," Fred said. "It took forever for me to learn how to face my own truth. I ran from it for years and years."

"It's hard," I said.

"The hardest," he said.

"Were you...?" I asked, the words dwindling off into space. I looked at him and he kept his head down, clasping his hands together.

Then he looked at me placidly and nodded. "Yes," he said. "Many times."

I felt tears building and I pinched my lips together and gazed out the window. "Cost me a lot," I said.

"It costs everything," Fred said. "It bankrupts us in every way. The lucky ones rebuild. There's a lot of those kids who never got that chance."

"I went back there," I said.

"I still do."

"Even now?"

"Every year. Just to lay tobacco down and try to find forgiveness."

"Did you find it?"

He took a drink and set his cup down slowly. "It's a long road," he said.

"I don't know if I can, you know? I don't know if I even want to."

"It's part of it," Martha said. "It took me a long, long time, and even now I don't know if I've truly done it. More like I just live my life here, and it heals me. Time. Distance. Not thinking about it."

"Did they rape everyone?" I asked.

There was a long silence. In the distance I could hear the sounds of the mill and a train. I waited and they both looked at the floor.

"It doesn't have to be sexual to be rape, Saul," Martha said.

"When they invade your spirit, it's rape too," Fred said.

I nodded. "That's how I felt. Invaded."

"And now?" Fred asked.

"Now I'm just tired of the way I've been living. I want something new built on something old. I wanted to come back. This is the only place I felt like something was possible for me. Don't know what I want to do. Just want to work on the idea of what's possible." I wrung my hands together and looked at them.

Fred reached over and took Martha's hand. They smiled at each other. "We hoped you would, some day," she said. "We all wanted to go out and find you, but we knew we couldn't. We knew you'd have to find your own way. The hardest part was that we knew how hard your road would be—but we had to let you go."

"They scooped out our insides, Saul. We're not responsible for that. We're not responsible for what happened to us. None of us are." Fred said. "But our healing—that's up to us. That's what saved me. Knowing it was my game."

"Could be a long game," I said.

"So what if it is?" he said. "Just keep your stick on the ice and your feet moving. Time will take care of itself."

"I know how to do that," I said.

"I know you do," he said.

53 ———

Virgil was a supervisor at the mine. He was married and had three boys. The days of the far-flung reserve tournaments had long gone, and there were Native teams in town leagues and amateur leagues across the North. As more Indian hockey players made the National Hockey League, it had become easier for Native kids to get on established teams. The reserve tournaments had evolved into huge annual tournaments in places like Thunder Bay, Sault Ste. Marie, Sudbury and Timmins. Those tourneys featured up to twenty-four teams, and the skill level was so impressive that big-league scouts were no longer oddities in the stands. The Moose had all grown up, married or moved away, and what remained of them was called the Manitouwadge Miners now. They played in a Senior B circuit and had yet to come close to a championship. But they were good. Fred filled me in on everything as we ate the lunch Martha prepared for us.

"You're only thirty-three, Saul," he said. "They could use you on the Miners."

"I haven't played since I left here. Haven't been on skates since then either."

"Talent like yours doesn't go away."

While we ate I told them about Father Leboutilier. I told them about how the game was the means of my emotional and mental survival. I told them how I could lose myself in it and how when I found I couldn't any longer, the joy I'd found and the elaborate cover it offered me both disappeared. They listened and nodded, and when I had finished we sat in a well of silence.

"So I think what I want to do is coach," I said finally. "Kids. Native kids. I want to bring them the joy I found; the speed, the grace, the strength and the beauty of the game. I want to give that back."

Martha smiled. "Virgil's looking for a coach. The mine sponsors a bantam team. Virgil's been trying to coach them, but it's hard to make time, with shift work and all."

"They're practicing tonight, if you want to have a look," Fred said.

"End of the season, isn't it?" I asked.

"Two more games. Still, you should take a look at the squad."

"Where?"

"Town built a big expensive arena a few years ago. You can't miss it. It's got a white roof you can see from most anywhere. I can drive you over."

"Think I'll walk. Be good to see the old town again."

"She ain't changed much. A few bigger stores, more people. But she's always been a mill and mining town and she'll never get away from that."

"Sounds perfect to me," I said.

54 ———

He was leaning on the boards, directing the players with a hockey stick. I could hear him shouting orders as soon as I stepped away from the concourse and began walking down the steps. His back was to me. It was a broad back. I took a seat fifteen rows up and watched him as he worked. He was like his father. He let them play the game, and he only whistled them to a stop when he had something specific to point out. They listened. They looked at him with their mouths open, down on one knee and breathing like stallions at the gate. He spoke in a low tone that I couldn't hear, but I remembered how the voice would sound, deep, rumbling, serious. When he'd made his point, they scrambled to their feet and took their positions and he blew the whistle and sent them into the high-speed whirl of the game.

They were fast. They had a lot more polish and they were a lot more acrobatic than kids had been when I was their age. They'd been well coached. Virgil ran them through a fast skating and passing drill that sent them up and down the ice in waves of three at a time. I could hear the excitement in their voices. After five minutes or so, he let them run through it on their own and they raced through the drill a half dozen times before he blew the whistle and called them to the bench. I moved a few rows closer so I could hear him.

"Full scrimmage now," he said. "But I want you coming out of your ends fast so there's no chance for the defense to bottleneck the neutral zone. Use your speed. Cut through the open ice and make yourself a strong target. I want those passes crisp and I want those rushes to end in a wrist shot from no further than fifteen feet out. No slappers, no dekes for now. Just set up the shot. Ready? Go!"

He skated to centre and dropped the puck and then drifted backwards to the boards and leaned on his elbows. The team was relentless. They flew up and down the ice smoothly, efficiently, and each rush was capped with a strong wrist shot. They skated a full ten minutes before I inched up behind him.

"Fifteen's a natural centre," I said. "He sees the ice too well to waste him on the wing."

He turned his head slightly and arched an eyebrow when he saw me. "He's a sawed-off little runt. The big boys'll take away his ice."

"Not if he uses that speed."

"Everyone's the same speed when they're flat on their back."

"Same size too," I said.

"Well, you'd know. Your whole career was spent on your back."

"You obviously missed the half when I was face down."

"Didn't. Just too sensitive to your feelings to want to mention it," Virgil said. "When did you get back?"

"Long enough for lunch and a talk with your folks."

"You look good."

"You wanna kiss me now or later?"

He snorted. "Think I'd as soon kiss the north end of a southbound moose."

"I was a Moose once."

He spun on his skates and leaned on the boards to look at me. He was stern when he spoke. "That seems like a long fuckin' time ago right now. I wanted to punch your lights out for leaving."

"Still want to do that?"

"Maybe," he said. "Depends on what you have to say for yourself. You want to get a beer and talk it out?"

"I don't drink. Not anymore. Used to. Didn't really work for me."

He nodded. "All right. I'm gonna get these guys into the dressing room and talk a little strategy. Why don't you wait for me outside? Ten minutes, tops."

"Okay," I said. I watched him bring the practice to a close and when he followed the players off the ice and into the walkway under the stands, he looked at me.

"Don't disappear again," he said.

"I won't. I'm there. Ten minutes, tops."

55

We settled for sitting in the stands while the rink man cleaned the ice. There was a long silence and I struggled to find words to break it. Virgil sat with his hands cupped in front of his face, staring straight ahead. I understood then how hard years are to get a hold of, how elusive the life in them can be to capture and retell. I understood then too that time does not heal all wounds. I wanted to say it all in one brilliantly executed sentence, encompass all of it in a succinct, effortless rush. But I couldn't. I was at a loss where to begin. In the end, he did it for me.

"You're one of those kids, aren't you? One of the ones the schools fucked up. My dad told me some of what he went through. When they said they wanted to bring you out of there, I guess I kinda knew why, even then. Knew it wasn't all about the game."

"I didn't know," I said. "Not for a long time. Not until just this past year."

"Jesus."

"Don't think he had anything to do with it, really."

He turned in his seat. "I know. I'm sorry. Crap choice of words."

He stared down at the ice while I told him about Father Leboutilier. I told him about my family and how I'd come to be at St. Jerome's. I told him about the rage that built in me that I had never understood and how it corroded everything, even the game. I told him about the road, the jobs, the towns, and then I told him about the booze.

"The ultimate device," I said. "It lets you go on breathing but not really living. It lets you move but not remember. It lets you do but not feel. I don't know why I fell into it so easily, why I lost myself so deep. I just thought I was crazy. But turns out I was just hurt, lonely, guilty, ashamed—and mostly just really, really sad."

"Did you want to hunt that fucker down? Make him feel some of the same pain?" Virgil asked. He still couldn't turn away from looking at the ice.

"At first, yeah. Then, the more we got into it at the centre the more I realized it was more than just him. I'd be hunting a long time if I lashed out at everyone. In the end, I learned the only one I could take care of was me."

He turned to me finally. His cheeks were slick with tears. "Five minutes alone in a room with each of them. That's what I'd wish for. For what they did to my dad, my mother, my grandparents, you. The fuckers."

"I know. It still hurts. It will for a long time. But I know that now. I know that and I have ways to deal with it. Better ways than running, abandoning people, fighting, drinking."

"Yeah? And what are those better ways?" He leaned back now and shunted so that he could half-face me.

"Come back here, for one thing. I always felt most like home here. Get a job. Work. There's a lot of healing to be had by picking up a lunch pail. Then I thought maybe I'd shop around for a team to coach.

He raised his eyebrows. "You're still young. You could play. Shit, the Miners could use you."

"They could use that other guy, Virgil. That bag of antlers with the speed and the moves. But I'm not that other guy anymore. I want to get back to the joy of the game. That's for sure. But if I learned anything while I was at the centre, it's that you reclaim things the most when you give them away. I want to coach. I mean, if I could get my hands on that number fifteen, I could turn him into something."

Virgil smiled. "That's my son. Billy. He's eleven, almost twelve, but he's skating with the bantams. Reminds me a lot of another speedster I once knew. He knows about you."

"He does? How?"

"You're a freakin' legend, Saul. No one ever played the game like you. Every guy who was on the Moose has told their kids about you."

"The guys are still around?"

"Not all of them. Most of them. They're all beer-bellied and fat now. Got a basketful of kids like I do, all married up and hog-tied, but we get together for shinny late at night sometimes when the ice is free. We talk about you."

"Think they'd want to see me?"

"We got ice tonight. Why don't you see for yourself?"

56 ———

The white glory of a rink. I found a used pair of skates at the sporting goods store and a good stick and I stood at the door to the player's bench looking out at the ice and trembling. I told Virgil that I needed some time to get my legs under me. He knew that I meant more than getting used to skating again. So he arranged to let me have the ice to myself for an hour before the guys showed up. I dressed on the bench. My head down lacing up my skates and my nose full of the smell of a rink. Wood. Sweat. Spit. Leather. When I stood and faced the ice itself, it was dazzling. I stood at the gate and it spread out in front of me as if it were its own special world—and it was. I knew its geography. I knew its breezes. I knew the chill of it. It took me five minutes before I could push off.

When I landed I couldn't move my feet. I glided straight across the ice to the opposite boards and gripped the top of them with my hands. Then I turned and leaned on them and just looked at the wide oval of ice. I pinched my lips together hard. I understood then that when you miss a thing it leaves a hole that only the thing you miss can fill. The feel of the rink on my face. I closed my eyes and pushed off from the boards. I turned lazily at centre and skated slowly around the red circle. Then I headed for the boards and pushed along them and around the end behind the net. When I turned up ice I pushed off harder. There was no rhythm. There was only the effort of propelling myself along.

There'd been a practice just before I'd arrived. Someone had left a wad of tape on the ice. When I reached it I scooped it up with the blade of my stick. It felt like a horse turd. I skated loosely from end to end with that ball of tape on my stick. Then I tucked it backwards between my legs and spun on one blade to pick it up and cradled it on the blade. I snapped it into the top corner of the net. I laughed then. I opened my mouth and I let myself peal off a great bray of laughter. Then I scooped up that wad of tape and began to move faster around that blazing white glory of ice.

I skated until sweat was pouring down my face. I skated until my legs became elastic and my breath was hard in my lungs. I didn't have anywhere near the speed I used to have, but I could still skate. When I bent to scoop the tape out of the goal, a real puck caromed around the bottom bar. I turned and Virgil was at the gate with Fred and Martha.

"Even up here in the sticks, we like to use a hockey puck to play hockey," Virgil said and pushed out onto the ice.

"Old habits," I said when he reached me.

"New days," he said.

"The guys here?"

"Them and more," he said.

"What do you mean?"

He waved his arm and Fred stepped out onto the ice. Behind him were five of the original Moose, still recognizable despite the years. Behind them were some kids of assorted ages and sizes and behind them were young girls and older women. Everyone had a hockey stick. They skated toward us in a wide stream and stood in a circle around us. Martha waved from the bench.

"Best way to choose up sides is the old-fashioned way," Stu Little Chief said with a nod to me. "Do the honours, Saul?"

"Sure," I said.

Everyone dropped their sticks in the centre-ice circle. I skated in and began pushing sticks toward each blue line. When they were all cleared from the centre, the teams were set. Virgil was on the opposite team. He skated to the faceoff circle.

I met him there. At least eighteen of us were on the ice.

"How are we gonna do this?" I asked.

"Gotta hit the post to call it a goal. No raising the puck."

"No, I mean with all these people. How are we gonna play the game?"

He smiled and tapped my stick with his. "Together," he said. "Like we shoulda all along."

I smiled. He won that first faceoff, but I didn't care.